The

Quiet

Reckoning

A.W. Collins

i

Copyright © 2026 A.W. Collins

All rights reserved

First Edition

A.W. Collins, Author

Prairieville, LA

ISBN 979-8-9951733-0-4 (paperback)

ISBN 979-8-9951733-1-1 (eBook)

First originally published by A.W. Collins 2026

CHAPTER 1

Shadows and Smoke

The porch light buzzed and flickered like it couldn't decide whether to stay alive or fizzle out and die too. Randy's body lay slumped beside the truck in the driveway. His limbs were twisted awkwardly beneath his lifeless body, and his mouth was slightly parted like the insult he'd been about to spew was still caught in his throat. Blood spread beneath him in a dark fan pattern, mixing with the gravel, the beer, and the night. Andy stood over it all with the bandana pulled down to his neck, and the gloves still tight around his fingers. His pulse was thundering, and his hands began to shake slightly. Many years of living in fear culminated in this single act of finality. He realized, at that moment, his life would never be the same. But he knew what had to happen next.

Andy moved swiftly but carefully, like he was being watched even though he wasn't. He bent over and pried open Randy's wallet. Inside was some cash, his ID, and some expired gas cards. He pocketed the cash and scattered the rest across the driveway. Then he opened the truck's glove compartment. He yanked it open roughly, leaving it hanging on its hinges. He opened the center console, rifled through it, and left it half-spilled. From the toolbox in the truck bed, he grabbed a wrench and tossed it near the porch steps. He kicked the front door in just a little; enough to make it look forced. He wanted to run, but he thought about what Eric had told him: *running gets noticed.* So, instead, he moved swiftly through the cover of darkness.

He crossed the street and slipped through the narrow break in the neighbors' chain-link fence. The woods behind the Everett's house hadn't changed much. The dirt path was still soft and worn, and the trees were thick and tall. He ducked under low limbs until he reached the clearing where the old oak stood. The oak tree. Their oak tree. He and Billy Jenkins had climbed it a thousand times. It had been everything from a pirate ship to a lookout tower. At times, they thought it was the top of the world. Now, it would be a grave.

Andy dropped to his knees and began digging with his hands. The soil was damp and stubborn. It was full of roots and old acorns. He didn't stop though. He was beginning to breathe heavily, but he didn't even think about what it meant. When the hole was deep enough, he pulled the revolver from his waistband. It was still warm. He wrapped it in the black bandana and dropped it into the hole. Then he covered it slowly and firmly, packing the earth tight over it. He smoothed it flat with the palms of his gloved hands and covered the disturbed ground with leaves and acorns. He rinsed the gloves in the rainwater that had collected in a small puddle next to the tree. He whispered something to himself that he couldn't even remember just a minute later. He stood and stared at the tree. The moonlight cut through the branches and painted shadows on the ground like scars. *You don't get to keep winning,* he thought. *Not anymore.*

On the way back to the shelter, Andy ditched the gloves in an old trash bin at the boarded-up abandoned gas station. He made it back to the shelter before the city woke up. He slipped through the side gate and up the stairwell without seeing a soul. The hallway was quiet. The kind of quiet that only existed between four and six in the morning. The door to their room creaked softly, but not enough to stir Marie. She was still curled under her blanket, breathing slowly with her back to the wall. Andy eased out of the windbreaker, kicked off the borrowed shoes, and slipped back under his sheet. He faced the wall like nothing had happened. His muscles were trembling under the calm, but his eyes stayed open. He was wide awake.

CHAPTER 2

Noise in the Dark

The call came in just after 6:00 a.m. A neighbor two doors down from Randy's house had gone out for a smoke before leaving for work and saw the shape in the driveway. At first, he thought it was a drunk who passed out cold. He walked over to get a closer look. As he approached Randy's lifeless body, he noticed a dark stain on the gravel beneath him. After another step closer, he realized it was blood. He called out once, "Hey buddy, are you ok?" There was no response. He called out again, "Hey pal, do you need help?" Still no response.

The first squad car arrived with lights only, no sirens. A uniformed officer crouched low beside the body, careful not to disturb the scene. He took one look at the body and radioed it in. By 6:30, the property was wrapped in yellow tape. Two more patrol cars pulled up; followed by an unmarked detective sedan. A pair of early joggers were waved off the sidewalk. Someone peeked from behind a curtain across the street. The day had barely started, and it had already gone sideways.

Detective Melinda Graves stepped out of her car with coffee in one hand and a tired expression on her face. She was in her forties, but her eyes carried the kind of wear that didn't come from age. It was the kind of wear that came from seeing too many things that didn't make sense. The uniformed officer briefed her quickly: Male, late forties, single gunshot to the chest, front yard in the gravel driveway. His wallet's been rifled through. The front door has been kicked in. The glovebox is open. It looks like a

4

robbery gone wrong. Graves shook her head and muttered, "Too clean," as she crouched beside the body. She scanned the porch, the grass, and the tire tracks in the gravel. "Find out if any neighbors heard the shot," she said. "Yes ma'am," the officer replied, "We'll get right on it."

Graves stood up, sipping from her coffee like it might help her think faster. She said, "Get Crime Scene out here. Bag and tag everything. Knock on every door for half a block." She stepped up to the porch. Her eyes landed on the tipped-over bottle and the splattered beer near the truck. She said, "The victim was out here before the shot. He didn't come out after. The killer was waiting…or watching." The officer nodded and asked, "You think it wasn't random?" Graves didn't answer right away. She just looked at the footprint on the door near the door frame. It was large, but narrow. "I think whoever did this knew where he'd be," she said.

Meanwhile back at the shelter, Andy lay motionless in bed. His adolescent mind was racing with thoughts of what would come next. The city was fully awake now. Sirens had howled once in the distance; then again. A low hum of traffic rolled past the shelter like background music to the morning routine. Marie stirred in her bed. She coughed twice and sat up with a wince. Andy didn't move. "You sleep okay?" she asked, rubbing her eyes. Andy blinked slowly and rolled to his side. "Yeah. Fine," he said. Marie smiled faintly, weak and cracked at the edges. She said, "Well, I think today's the day we talk to that social worker again. We might get a case manager lined up. And maybe even look at the housing list." Andy nodded and said, "That'd be good." He knew she was trying to sound hopeful. She was trying to be normal, but he could see it. Something just didn't seem right with her. She'd lost a little weight. The random pains in her abdomen weren't going away. Sometimes she moved like she hurt in places she wasn't ready to name yet.

Marie stood and crossed the room to the window. She tilted the blinds with two fingers and glanced at an angle around the wall of the building next door. She saw a couple police units fly by with lights flashing. "Huh," she said after a moment. "They seemed to be in hurry to get somewhere." Andy swung his legs over the side of the bed and stood up. He kept his face calm and his hands steady despite the heavy burden he had suddenly thrust upon himself. "Want me to grab us some breakfast?" he asked. Marie nodded while rubbing her forehead. "Yeah. That'd be nice," she said. As he left the room and made his way down the narrow shelter hallway, Andy caught sight of himself in the dusty mirror on the wall. His eyes were rimmed with shadows, but there was no guilt there. There was just the echo of everything he couldn't say. On his way to school that morning, he quickly, but discreetly placed the windbreaker and the borrowed shoes back in the donation bin where he and Eric had found them just days earlier.

By noon, word had spread. Randy Guillaume, a former Navy firefighter, part-time auto mechanic, and full-time bully was dead. Shot in his own yard. No witnesses. No video footage. No sign of a forced struggle inside the house. Just a scene that felt...staged. Detective Graves sat in her car scrolling on her laptop computer. She found a copy of a police report previously filed at Randy's address. It was one from a few years ago, a domestic disturbance with his wife, Marie Guillaume. No charges were filed, but there were bruises on her arms. The report noted a minor child in the home. A male child. He was ten or eleven at the time. There was no follow-up. She stared at the report, then back at the house. "Pull up current addresses for Marie Guillaume," she said into her phone, "See if she's still local." A voice crackled through, "She was recently placed in temporary shelter housing in Baton Rouge." "Get me the address," she replied.

Graves didn't know what she expected to find. Maybe nothing. Maybe just the shadow of something she couldn't quite pinpoint yet. But if there was one thing she'd learned in all her years chasing ghosts, it was this: People like Randy Guillaume rarely died by accident. And sometimes the quiet ones knew more than they let on.

CHAPTER 3

What They Don't Say

Detective Graves arrived at the shelter just before 2:00 p.m. She didn't wear her badge around her neck like some officers did. It stayed clipped inside her blazer pocket, heavy but invisible. She believed in subtlety. She believed in less intimidation and more conversation. People would typically say more when they forgot you were the law.

The shelter sat tucked between a boarded-up dry cleaner and a forgotten warehouse with busted windows. The paint on the building was chipped, and the sign out front hung slightly crooked. A place like this wasn't meant to be noticed. It was built to disappear in plain sight. Graves stepped through the front door and into the scent of industrial cleaner and overcooked soup. The volunteer at the desk, a girl in her early twenties with a messy bun and exhausted eyes, looked up, startled. "Hi," Graves said gently, "I'm looking for a Marie Guillaume. I was told she's staying here?" The volunteer blinked and reached for a clipboard, "Is this about the housing application? I think she was waiting for..." "I'm with the police department," Graves said softly, flashing her ID just enough to be seen, "It's not about her. I just need to ask her a couple of questions. Nothing urgent." The girl hesitated, then said, "Let me check with the supervisor." Graves nodded and waited. Her eyes drifted across the room. She saw kids coloring with broken crayons, a woman sleeping upright in a chair, and another woman trying to fix a busted zipper on her coat with a safety pin. She saw people surviving in the quietest way they could. After a few minutes, the volunteer returned and said,

"Marie's in the common room. You can talk to her there if it's quick."

Graves followed her down a short hallway into a small open room where the television hummed softly in the background. Marie sat alone on a faded green couch, sipping from a chipped mug. She looked older than her file said. She looked frailer too. Her skin was pale, and her eyes were sunken. She looked like someone who hadn't had a full night's sleep in years. "Marie Guillaume?" Graves asked. Marie turned and nodded slowly, "That's me." Graves offered a soft smile and extended her hand as she said, "Detective Melinda Graves. Sorry to bother you. Just following up on something. Do you have a minute?" Marie glanced down at her mug, then back up, "Sure." Graves sat on the adjacent chair. "It's about Randy," she said. The blank look on Marie's face didn't change. She didn't blink or flinch. She just stared straight ahead. "What about him?" she asked flatly. Graves said, "There's no easy way to tell you this. He was found dead early this morning. A gunshot wound to his chest. Outside his house." Marie's lips parted slightly, but no sound came out at first. The shock of what she had just heard muted her. After a few seconds of silence, she said anxiously, "Dead?" "Yes, ma'am, dead. I'm sorry," said Graves. Marie set her mug down. Her hands were shaking just enough to make the porcelain clink against the table. She said, "I...I hadn't heard." "I figured," Graves said as she leaned forward slightly, "I know some of your history with him. There's a report from a few years ago. No charges were filed, but it was noted you had bruises." Marie nodded faintly and said, "He...hurt me for a long time." "Was he still bothering you recently?" Graves asked. Marie hesitated then said, "Not directly. We left. We got out a few weeks ago. I haven't seen or heard from him since." "Do you know anyone who might have wanted to hurt him?" Graves asked. Marie met her eyes just then and said, "A lot of people probably did. He ran around on me for years. Maybe one of his girlfriends had a husband or a boyfriend who did it. He wasn't a good man." Graves gave a slight nod and said, "Do you mind if I ask where you were last night?" Marie looked startled. "You think I did it?" she said anxiously. "Just a standard question," Graves said calmly. "We ask everyone who had history with the victim." "I was here," Marie said. "I was asleep. Ask the staff. Ask my son." Graves tilted her head slightly, "Your son?" "Yes, Andy. He's thirteen. He's in school right now," Marie said. Graves jotted the name in her notebook. Then asked, "And you're sure he was here too?" Marie's brow stiffened, "Of course. We share a room. He didn't leave. He was here all night." Graves smiled politely and said, "Alright. That's all I have for now. If you think of anything that might be helpful, please give us a call. Thank you for your time."

Marie picked her mug back up; her grip was so tight her knuckles turned white. Graves stood and walked out of the room without further comment. But as she reached the front desk again, she turned to the volunteer and asked, "The boy, Andy. He's in school?" The girl nodded, "Yes, ma'am. He goes to the middle school over on Pine Street." Graves tapped her pen as she asked, "Ever notice anything...unusual? Has he had trouble here?" The girl looked unsure when she said, "Not really. He's a quiet kid. He doesn't talk much. Mainly keeps to himself." "Does he ever leave unexpectedly? Wander off?" asked Graves. She shook her head, "Not that I've seen. He's usually in the room or with his mom. Kind of...a loner. He stays out of everyone's way." Graves nodded and placed her card on the counter as she said, "If you think of anything, or if he says something odd, anything at all, call me." Then she stepped back into the afternoon sun, pulled out her notebook, and drew a line under Andy's name.

Marie sat in the common room long after Graves had gone. The tremble in her hands hadn't stopped. Her breaths were shallow. She felt something terrible closing in. It was a slow, creeping sense that the walls weren't just old, they were listening…and watching. When Andy returned from school, she pulled him aside. "A detective came to see me," she said. Andy's face froze. Then suddenly, he said, "What?" With mild panic in her voice, Marie said, "She said Randy's dead. He got shot. She asked where we were last night." Andy blinked rapidly as he asked, "How? By who? What did you tell her?" "I told her the truth," Marie said, watching him carefully. "That we were here all night. That you never left." Andy swallowed hard but said nothing. Marie leaned in close and lowered her voice, "Andy…if there's anything you haven't told me, now's the time." His eyes locked on her eyes for a moment. "There's nothing," he said. Marie wanted to believe him. But the quiet that followed wasn't just silence, it was heavy. It was like something unsaid had just walked between them and sat down to stay.

CHAPTER 4

The Oak Tree

The woods behind the Everett house were barely woods at all. It was just a ragged strip of trees dividing two neighborhoods that had seen better days. Trash collected beneath the leaves, and graffiti marked the trunks like teenage confessions. But to Andy, that patch of land was sacred. It was where he used to pretend the world made sense. Where the oak tree stood like a monument to another life. Fourteen steps from the fence line. Six more steps past the old tire swing stump. In between the "V" shape made by two roots at the base of the trunk, the revolver lay buried now; wrapped in a black bandana, beneath a mound of damp earth, leaves and rotten acorns.

He hadn't gone back since he buried the gun there; not even once. But it haunted him like the last breath before a scream. Every time he closed his eyes, he saw the way moonlight sliced through the branches and fell across the fresh soil. He also remembered how his hands shook, not from fear, but from certainty. There was no hesitation when he pulled the trigger. Only the sound of Randy's body hitting the gravel and the silence that followed. The kind of silence that didn't come from peace, but from finality. Andy had learned to deal with the anxiety that came with growing up in an abusive home, but the anxiety he had now was a new type of anxiety. It was due to the uncertainty of what was to come. It was a weight that was already becoming unbearable.

The Quiet Reckoning

At the shelter, days passed like a dull hum in the background. Nothing loud, and nothing sharp; just time stretching itself thin. Andy kept mostly to himself. He read when he could, drew in his notebook when he couldn't. He tried everything to keep his mind off what he had done. Lately, his drawings had changed. There were fewer knives and swords, and more empty fields and storm clouds. A figure sometimes showed up in the corner of the page, always small, and always turned away. Marie had grown quieter again as well. The abdominal pains came more often, and her movements were slower, like her body was listening to something dark inside it. Andy watched her closely, knowing she was watching him too. They now live in a kind of delicate balance. They were two survivors tiptoeing around the truth they both carried. They didn't speak much about that night. Not directly. But the silence between them had taken shape now. It pressed around the edges of every conversation. A weight that made even small talk feel fragile.

One afternoon, Marie returned from a meeting with the case manager. Her face looked pale. It was the kind of paleness that didn't come from lack of sleep alone. She sat across from Andy and pulled her sweater tighter around her. "They think we might have a housing lead," she said in a soft voice. "It's still early, but...maybe in a month or two." Andy nodded. "That's good," he said. Marie hesitated, then asked, "You doing okay?" Andy looked at her and said, "I'm fine." A second passed. Then another. "They still don't have any suspects," she said, watching him carefully. "The news said it was probably a robbery." Andy didn't flinch. He said, "Guess that's what it looked like." Marie studied his face with her lips pressing together like she was holding back something dangerous.

Finally, she leaned in and lowered her voice. "I need to know something," she said, "And I need you to tell me the truth." Andy's face went blank. "If the police come back," she continued, "and they start asking more questions...is there anything they might find? Anything that could lead to you?" His eyes drifted to the window. The sun was low, bleeding orange light across the sky. He hesitated, but then it came out suddenly. "I was careful," he said quietly. Marie was stunned by his quiet admission. "That's not what I'm asking," she said. Andy turned back to her and said, "I didn't leave anything behind." She stared at him for a long time, like she was searching for something just beneath his skin. Then she whispered, "Is it still out there? The gun?" Andy nodded once. At that moment, she realized her quiet little boy was no more. Marie looked down at her hands. They were trembling slightly. "Where is it?" she asked. "I can't tell you," he said, "Not yet anyway." Tears welled up in her eyes, but she blinked them away. "You have to tell me," she said. "You're still a child, Andy. This shouldn't be your burden to carry alone." "Then why did I have to be the one to stop him?" he asked, "Why did no one else do it?" Marie didn't have an answer. She only had guilt and fear. She had a slow-burning plan beginning to take shape in the back of her mind. She pressed Andy harder for an answer. After several minutes of silence, Andy whispered, "Do you remember the oak tree in the woods behind the Everett's house? The one me and Billy used to climb?" Marie nodded. Andy continued, "There's a "V" shape between two roots under the big branch. It's buried there. It's wrapped in a black bandana." Marie nodded again without saying a word. She felt relieved and worried at the same time. Later that night, while Andy was asleep, Marie sat alone in the common room with a paper cup of tea and a folded blanket pulled up over her knees. Her body ached in places she hadn't admitted yet. Her skin had grown thinner; her energy was less certain. But it wasn't just sickness that haunted her. It was the possibility of losing Andy to something far worse than poverty or illness. She had lived under Randy's shadow for too many years. She watched him break things like furniture, trust, and bones. She had always told herself she was doing the best she could. That surviving was enough. But Andy had made a different choice. A much harder one. And he had done it for both of them. She believed she could still fix this. If the police came closer, if Detective Graves returned with evidence or suspicion, Marie already knew what she'd say. She'd lead them to that tree herself. She'd give them the location, unwrap the buried gun with her own hands, and tell them exactly what they wanted to hear. She had killed Randy. He was drunk, she would say. He came after her one last time. She found the gun in the glovebox. She panicked. She pulled the trigger. And no one would doubt it because everyone already believed she had reason. She looked toward the hallway that led to the room where Andy was sleeping and whispered, "You won't carry this, baby. Not if I can help it."

CHAPTER 5

Pressure Points

Detective Graves didn't bother with backup. She didn't need it. She arrived at the shelter just after lunch, dressed in plain clothes. There was no badge around her neck, and no uniformed officer at her side. She figured if she showed up looking like the cavalry, the walls would go up faster than she could ask a question. The receptionist at the front desk, a young woman with bright eyes and chipped purple nail polish, buzzed her through with a hesitant smile. She said, "You're here to see Marie, right?" Graves nodded and said, "And her son, Andy." "She's in the common room. I'll let her know…" she said. "No," Graves said, gentle but firm. "Please don't. I'd rather talk to Andy first. One-on-one." The receptionist blinked, then nodded slowly and hesitantly said, "Okay, third door on the left." Graves knew it was risky speaking to a juvenile without a parent present, but she was willing to take the risk.

Graves made her way down the narrow hallway; her footsteps were softened by the worn linoleum. She passed a playroom with two toddlers sharing a broken toy firetruck. There was a bulletin board on the wall with job postings and a sign-up sheet for donated clothing. She hesitated for a moment at the bulletin board. She checked for Andy and Marie's names on the sign-up sheet but didn't see either one. When she made it to the door she looked inside. Andy sat alone at the corner table. Same spot as always, same notebook open in front of him. Only this time, he wasn't drawing. He was just staring at the page. He didn't flinch when Graves stepped in. He didn't look up right away either. He just waited. "You Andy?" she asked. He nodded. "I'm Detective Graves," she said as she sat down across from him without waiting for permission. "Can we talk for a few minutes?" she asked. Andy closed the notebook slowly and met her eyes, "About what?" Graves raised her eyebrows. He didn't smile. He didn't move. He was still, the way kids get only when they've learned stillness is safer than words. "How was your relationship with Randy?" she asked, "Did y'all get along?" Andy nodded as he said, "Sometimes." Graves leaned forward and asked, "Did he ever hit you?" Andy's voice was flat when he responded, "I don't know." Graves quickly snapped back, "You don't know if he hit you or not?" Andy looked at her with subtle defiance and said, "I don't remember him hitting me." She nodded slightly and said, "I see." She continued, "If he did ever hurt you, I can understand why you might want to hurt him back." Andy didn't blink as he stared at her. Graves studied him for a long time and thought: *You've got a good poker face kid. I'll give you that. But you're just a kid and kids make mistakes.* She said, "Sometime stories are told to cover holes. And sometimes we carry guilt that doesn't belong to us." Andy's hands were curled in his lap. "I'm not telling a story," he said. Graves waited. Silence filled the room. She let it stretch long enough to feel like a question. Finally, she said, "Do you know if Randy owned a gun?" Andy hesitated a moment and said, "I know he had one." "Did he ever use it to scare you? Or your mother?" Graves asked. Andy's jaw twitched as he said, "No." Graves nodded slowly, letting that answer sink in. She took a softer tone, "I've read the reports, Andy. The bruises on your mother, the ER visits with no follow-up, and the neighbors who heard yelling but didn't want to get involved. Your mom said y'all left him a few weeks ago, but we both know a man like that doesn't let go easy." Andy still offered no response. She tried a new angle. "Listen," she said, "We're not out to ruin yours or your mom's life. That's not what this is. But someone's dead and I have to figure out who did it. And if that someone was trying to protect you, or if you were trying to protect someone else, now's the time to say it." Andy's voice came low and final, "I didn't kill him." Graves didn't flinch. She leaned back in her chair and let out a quiet sigh, "Okay. I hope you didn't." She stood up, smoothing her blazer and said, "Just know this...if you change your mind, I'm around. And I listen better than most people think I do." Graves walked slowly toward the door. Andy watched her as she exited the room.

That night, Marie doubled over in the hallway outside the laundry room. It was the third time that week. The pain started like a cramp and bloomed outward like a fist tightening around her entire torso. She clutched the doorframe with one hand and pressed the other against her stomach. She didn't scream. She'd learned how to hold that in a long time ago. Trina, the night volunteer, saw her double over in pain. "Marie! Are you okay?" she asked. Marie waved her off. "I'm fine," she said, "I'll be okay in a few minutes." She wasn't sure what was going on, exactly, but she knew it wasn't getting any better. She knew she needed to see a doctor, but she feared what she might find out. This was not the time for her to become sick. Andy needed her now more than ever.

CHAPTER 6

The Waiting Room

The clinic was quiet in that sterile, uneasy way that made Marie's skin itch. Everything smelled like antiseptic and unasked questions. The vinyl seats stuck slightly to the backs of her thighs, and the whispers scattered throughout the waiting room was the only thing keeping her from hearing the thump of her own heart. She'd been waiting for almost an hour, alone. Andy didn't even know she had an appointment. She told him she had a meeting with the case manager. It wasn't exactly a lie, but it wasn't the truth either. Across from her, a mother bounced a crying baby on her knee while a man with a swollen ankle filled out paperwork with a shaking hand. Everyone looked like they wanted to be anywhere else, but there. Marie didn't blame them.

A nurse in pale blue scrubs stepped into the waiting room and called her name softly, "Marie Guillaume?" Marie stood slowly. Her legs ached, and her stomach twisted as if it already knew what was coming. She led her down a narrow hallway lined with closed doors and motivational posters; "Health is Wealth," one read in bold cheerful lettering. Another had a sunflower blooming under the words *You Are Not Alone*. But Marie had never felt more alone in her life. The exam room was cold. The paper on the table crinkled when she sat. The nurse checked her blood pressure, took her temperature, asked a few routine questions with the mechanical detachment of someone who'd asked them a thousand times. Then she left, promising the doctor would be in shortly. Marie stared at the closed door and tried not to pick at her fingernails. She'd told herself this was just precautionary. It was just a check-up. Just a few tests to rule things out. But deep down, she knew. She'd known for months. The weight loss. The fatigue. The dull, twisting pain in her abdomen. The blood. She had explained it away for a long time as being too much stress, or not enough food. Maybe it was just an ulcer. But the body has a way of telling the truth, even when the mind refuses to hear it.

The door opened, and Dr. Fallon entered. A tall, soft-spoken woman with warm brown eyes and a clipboard tucked under one arm. Marie had seen her twice before. She liked her. She trusted her, even. But the moment their eyes met, Marie's chest tightened. The doctor's face was calm, but it wasn't the calm of someone bringing good news. It was the kind of calm that comes after bad news has already landed. Dr. Fallon pulled the stool closer and sat down. "Marie," she said gently, "Thanks for coming in." Marie nodded but didn't speak. After a quick examination, Dr. Fallon said, "We need to run some tests." Marie kept her hands tucked between her legs, gripping the edge of the paper-covered table. "Okay," she said, "What kind of tests?" "We will start with some simple blood tests and a CT scan and go from there," Dr. Fallon said. Marie nodded. The doctor continued, "Wait here and the nurse will be back to draw some blood. Then we will get you over to imaging." Marie's stomach was in knots at this point. She just nodded with angst written all over her face. After having blood drawn and the CT scan was completed, Marie returned to the shelter and tried her best to act as if everything were alright as she waited for her test results.

A few days later, Marie received a call from Dr. Fallon's nurse. The nurse said, "Marie, we need you to come into the office today at 10:00 a.m. We have the results of your blood tests and CT scan. Dr. Fallon would like to speak to you." With fear in her voice, Marie said, "Okay, I'll be there." When she arrived at the clinic, she was taken immediately to a consultation room. This was not going to be good news. Marie felt it in her bones. A few minutes later Dr. Fallon walked into the room. Marie was as nervous as she had ever been in her life. "There's no easy way to say this, so I'm going to be honest with you," Dr. Fallon said. "You have cancer. It's colon cancer, and based on the imaging, it's advanced." Marie blinked. She felt the words before she understood them. "How advanced?" she asked. Her voice was thinner than she expected. The doctor paused then said, "Stage four. It's spread to your liver and possibly to your lymph nodes." Marie stared at the floor. Her ears buzzed. Dr. Fallon said, "We'll need to run more tests to confirm the exact extent, but the primary tumor is significant. It's likely been growing for some time." "How long do I have?" Marie asked, still staring at the floor. "It's hard to say," Dr. Fallon replied. "With treatment, chemo and maybe targeted therapies, you could have more time. Some patients live for several years with the right support. But without treatment…" her voice trailed off. Marie nodded slowly, "We live in a shelter," she said, "I don't have insurance." Dr. Fallon looked down at her clipboard. "There are some programs," she said. "State aid, hospital charity options. We can connect you with a social worker to help navigate that. You deserve to fight this, Marie." Marie looked up at her for the first time. Her eyes were dry, but something deeper cracked inside her. She wasn't afraid to die. Not really. But she was afraid of what her death would leave behind. "Can I ask you something?" she said. "Of course," replied the doctor. "If someone…someone you loved more than anything, did something terrible because they thought they were protecting you…would you protect them back? Even if it cost you the time you had left?" The doctor blinked. "I'm not sure I understand." Marie gave a tired smile and said, "You don't have to."

The rest of the appointment was a blur. Lots of paperwork, referrals, and the promise of a call from a caseworker. Marie moved through it all like a ghost, her body in one place and her thoughts somewhere else entirely. Outside the clinic, the afternoon was warm and indifferent. People moved along the sidewalk like nothing had changed, but everything had. She walked slowly; each step was deliberate. The ache in her side was worse today. She wondered how much longer she could hide it from Andy. He was sharp; too sharp for his own good. But she needed him to believe things were okay, at least for a little while longer. She needed time. Not time to live, but time to make a decision. Because the clock had started ticking. Not just on her life, but on how far she was willing to go to save his.

CHAPTER 7

Smoke But No Fire

Detective Melinda Graves sat in her unmarked sedan, parked half a block from the scene of the murder that had been making the rounds on every department whiteboard for over a week now. Randy Guillaume, former Navy firefighter, part-time mechanic, full-time domestic nuisance, was dead. One gunshot to the chest. Clean and quiet. There were no signs of a struggle inside, no defensive wounds, and no witnesses. A robbery, maybe. But it was a neat one. And Graves' experience says it was too neat.

She'd spent the last several days peeling back the layers of his life, and what she found was exactly what she expected: a trail of bitterness, broken relationships, and angry lovers. Randy had a bad reputation. He was cruel, charming, and just dangerous enough to draw in women who mistook danger for charisma. Graves had tracked down three of them so far. One named Lisa worked nights at a dive bar off Government Street. She still had a mark on her jaw from two months ago. She said Randy backhanded her because he was jealous of one of her regular customers at the bar. She said she hadn't seen him since that altercation. No report was filed. Another, named Carla, claimed she hadn't seen him in nearly a year but refused to look Graves in the eye. The third was a married woman named Gina. She had a husband with a criminal record and a short temper. That seemed promising, but only for about an hour. Graves met with the husband in his driveway. He worked at an auto mechanic shop and had grease under his nails and rage in his voice.

He said he knew all about Randy, had even threatened to beat him up once. But the night of the murder, he'd been at a poker game with four buddies and a fridge full of Miller Lite. The poker game lasted into the early morning hours. His alibi was confirmed. Graves made the calls and checked the timeline. It was airtight. Lead after lead fizzled. No fingerprints. No weapon. No witnesses. Just a dead man and a scene that felt like it had been written for television. She stood now on the edge of the gravel driveway, staring at the dark patch where the blood had dried. She didn't believe in perfect crimes. But she did believe in purpose, and whoever killed Randy had a very specific reason for it.

Back at the station, Graves sat with her notes spread across her desk like puzzle pieces. She'd circled Marie's name three times now, and underlined Andy's once. The shelter visits had stuck with her. Marie's face when she learned about Randy's death was too still. Her answers seemed too somber. And Andy...something about the boy nagged at her. He was too calm. Kids didn't usually hide things that well. They'd usually crack under a little pressure. They would tremble with fear of the consequences. But not him. He looked like someone who had already been cracked and hardened long before this ever happened.

She pulled up Andy's school file again. He had a clean record. He had good grades when he'd been enrolled steadily. But there were a lot of gaps. There were lots of transfers too. Teacher comments marked him as quiet, intense, but polite. One note stood out: *"Andy tends to dissociate during conflict. Very mature emotionally, but distant."* Graves closed the file and leaned back in her chair. Something was off. She could feel it. It was like a voice whispering under all the noise: *You're looking in the wrong places.*

She opened a drawer and pulled out the domestic report from three years ago. The one involving Marie and Randy. No charges were filed, but the responding officer's notes were detailed: bruises, smashed picture frame, child present; male, approximately ten years old. Andy. He was old enough to remember and old enough to understand. Graves stood, grabbed her keys, and headed back out.

The shelter smelled like bleach and stale bread. Graves flashed her badge again at the desk. Same volunteer, different day. The girl gave a half-smile and buzzed her through. Marie was in the common room again, sipping lukewarm tea and staring at a daytime talk show with the volume off. She looked even thinner than last time. Graves noticed it immediately. She had sunken cheeks, shadows under her eyes, and her skin was too pale. "Detective Graves," Marie said softly, setting her cup down. "Mind if we talk a moment?" Graves asked, politely, but firm. Marie nodded and followed her into a quieter hallway near the staff office. "Just a few follow-ups," Graves began, "I appreciate your patience." Marie nodded again and said, "Of course." Graves pulled out her notebook and asked, "Do you remember the last time you spoke to Randy?" Marie looked down and said, "The day before we left. He came home drunk and angry. Same as always." "Did he threaten you?" Graves asked. Marie didn't answer right away. "He always threatened me," she finally said, "That was the air we breathed in that house." Graves nodded, "Did he suspect you were planning to leave?" "No," Marie said quickly, "I made sure of that." "You're sure?" asked Graves. Marie's face stiffened, "Yes." Graves paused, then asked, "And your son, Andy. Did he ever say anything about Randy in the last few weeks? Anything about wanting to go back? Or...to settle things?" Marie's shoulders rose, then fell slowly. "Andy's a good kid," she said, "He doesn't talk about Randy. He doesn't need to." Graves looked at her. Really looked at her and said, "Marie, I'm going to be honest with you. We've ruled out every other possible suspect. The people Randy was involved with, none of their stories hold water, but their alibis do. Which leaves me circling back." Marie's lips parted, but she didn't speak. Graves continued, "I don't want to come at this from the wrong angle. I'm not accusing anyone. But I need to know if you're protecting someone. Because if you are...that never ends the way people hope it will." Marie blinked once. Then she said, "I have nothing and no one to protect." The silence stretched thin. "Alright," Graves said, tucking her notebook away, "We'll be in touch."

As she left the shelter, she didn't feel satisfaction. She felt tension. It was like a string being pulled tighter with every word unsaid. She no longer thought Marie had pulled the trigger. But she was starting to believe she knew who did.

CHAPTER 8

Fractures in the Silence

Andy hadn't been sleeping much lately. He only pretended to. He closed his eyes when Marie did. He turned his face toward the wall and stayed still. But every night, he lay awake, listening to the wheeze in her breaths, the occasional cough she muffled into her blanket or pillow, and the silence that followed like a warning. Something was wrong with her. He'd known it before she said anything. The way her skin had gone pale and almost gray. The way she pressed her hand to her stomach when she thought he wasn't looking. The way her voice trembled even when her words didn't. She hadn't told him she went to the doctor, but she didn't need to. Andy could tell something had changed the moment she walked back into the shelter that afternoon. Her eyes were hollow, not just tired but distant. Her steps were slower. Her hands trembled when she thought he wasn't watching. But he always was. She was slowly slipping away. And now, Detective Graves was circling closer.

At school, Andy kept his head down. He sat in the back, finished his work quickly, and avoided the lunch table altogether. He didn't talk unless someone forced him to. And even then, he said just enough to be left alone. He caught whispers, sometimes, of teachers in the hallway. Something about a detective asking questions. Not questions about him, directly, but questions about his family. Questions about Marie. Questions about "the boy." They didn't say his name, but Andy could feel it hanging in the air like smoke.

That afternoon, when he got back to the shelter, Marie was waiting for him near the stairwell. She didn't smile. She just stood there, thin as a shadow with her arms crossed tight over her chest. "She came back," she said, "Detective Graves." Andy's stomach dropped. "What'd she want this time?" he asked. "She's asking more questions. Digging into the past. Digging into Randy's...affairs and our fights. She asked about the night we left. She's circling the fire." Andy stayed quiet. He could feel the tremble rising in his chest, but he wouldn't let it reach his face. Marie looked at him with glassy eyes and said, "She asked about you." He blinked and asked, "What'd you say?" Marie hesitated, then said, "That you were with me. That you didn't know anything." Andy nodded slowly, "Okay." But something in her voice made his skin go cold. She was starting to sound like she was worried Detective Graves was beginning to get too close.

That night, he couldn't take it anymore. While Marie slept, curled beneath the thin blanket with one arm draped across her stomach, Andy slipped out of bed and sat on the floor near the window. He pressed his forehead to the cool glass and stared down at the alley behind the shelter. It wasn't fair. She'd endured everything. The fists, the fear, the running, and the bruises that never quite healed. And now...this? It haunted him like a broken heart; constant, quiet, and always there. The weight of what he'd done. The finality of it. He hadn't cried when he pulled the trigger. He had no regrets when he buried the gun. He told himself it was justice. He told himself it had to be done. He told himself that nobody else would stop Randy, not the courts, not the cops, not time. But now Graves was closing in. Marie was withering, and Andy was no longer sure he had saved anyone. He thought of the oak tree, the way the moonlight had sliced through its branches like silver knives. He thought of Billy Jenkins and how they used to pretend it was a fortress, a place where no one could ever find them. But someone always did.

The next morning, Marie barely touched her breakfast. She pushed eggs around her plate with a fork until the volunteer took the tray away. Andy sat across from her, chewing slowly, watching her every move. "I need to tell you something," she said quietly, not looking at his eyes. Andy stopped chewing. She continued, "I'm...not well. The doctor said it's bad. Stage 4 Cancer." He already knew something was wrong, but hearing it made his throat go dry. He forced himself to speak with tears in his eyes. "It can be treated, right?" he asked, "Stage 4 is bad, huh?" Marie nodded. Andy said, "How long before..." Marie interrupted, "They don't know. A few months. Maybe a year. If I get treatment." "Are you? You have to," he said abruptly. Marie didn't answer right away. After a few seconds she said, "There'll be more tests, more paperwork, and money we don't have." Andy stared at her long and hard and asked, "Why didn't you tell me?" "I didn't want to scare you," she replied. "I'm not scared," he said, too quickly. She looked at him then. Really looked at him. She said, "Yes, you are. But you've learned how to hide it. It's okay to be scared, son. I'm scared too." They sat in silence. Then she reached across the table and placed her hand over his. Her fingers were very thin. They were just bones under the skin. "Listen to me," she said, "Whatever happens next...you don't say a word. Not to anyone. Especially not to that detective." Andy's eyes locked onto hers as he asked, "Are you planning to do something?" "I plan on protecting you," she said. "You don't have to," he replied. "Yes," she said, squeezing his hand harder, "I do."

That night, Andy stayed awake again, watching the shadows on the ceiling. The shelter buzzed with muffled arguments, creaking beds, and the faint static of someone's radio two rooms over, but none of it reached him. Because he knew something was coming. He wasn't sure exactly what was coming, but Graves wasn't letting this go and neither was his mother.

CHAPTER 9

Confession Letter

Marie sat by the window in the room at the shelter with a pen gripped tight in her hand. Her hand was trembling slightly from the medication she had been taking for pain. Outside, the shelter parking lot was dimly lit under the soft moon light shining through the trees. Beyond that, the city exhaled its restless breath. Cars were moving and people were rushing home, unaware that a woman was scribbling the most important words of her life behind these walls. The medication dulled the edges of her pain but sharpened the urgency. Every hour felt like a countdown. Every moment of nausea, every new ache in her ribs was a reminder that her clock wasn't just ticking, it was winding down. She flipped open the small notebook Trina had given her and began to write:

To Whom It May Concern,

I, Marie Guillaume, am writing this statement freely and without coercion. This letter is my full confession to the death of Randall Thomas Guillaume, who was found shot and killed outside his residence on the night of March 27, 1999...

Her pen stopped for a moment. The words looked too clean on the page. They were too polite for the mess they were trying to contain. She exhaled, pushed through the fog of fatigue, and kept going:

I was the one who took the revolver from his drawer the night I left. I was the one who returned to that house. And I was the one who pulled the trigger. I was afraid. I knew Randy would never stop. He told me he'd find us, hurt us, and burn our lives to the ground. I believed him…

Marie paused again. Her thumb was trembling along the edge of the paper. She pictured Andy curled in his bed, sleeping like he used to when he was five and still believed monsters could be locked out with a nightlight. She pictured the way he'd gone quiet lately. The way he had looked over his shoulder even when no one was following. She had to do this:

I acted alone. My son, Andy, had no part in it. He did not know what I planned, and he did not accompany me that night. If any evidence suggests otherwise, it is wrong. He was a child trying to escape a violent home. He should not be punished for what I did to protect us both…

She gritted her teeth and forced herself to keep going. Now, her hand was cramping hard from the pressure of every stroke:

I accept full responsibility. I am prepared to speak further with law enforcement if needed, but I want it known clearly that this was my doing. Let this serve as the final account. I am not proud of what I did. But I am no longer afraid.

She signed her name with shaking fingers:

Marie Guillaume

April 22, 1999

The date blurred on the paper as a tear landed squarely over the "1" in the year. She wiped her face, folding the letter slowly and placing it in an envelope. She wrote one name on the front: Detective Melinda Graves. Then she tucked the envelope inside the drawer beside her bed. Her mind was made up. If it came down to Andy being charged with Randy's murder or being free, she was prepared to take full responsibility.

The next morning, when Andy rolled over, Marie was already sitting on the edge of her cot. She hadn't slept at all. He glanced over at her and she smiled. She was pale and small, but still his mother. Her hair was thinning. Her skin looked almost translucent, but her eyes were clear. She motioned for him to sit on the edge of her cot. "You okay?" she asked. Andy shrugged and said, "I guess so. Just worried about you." "Don't worry about me, baby," she said. "Everything is going to be okay," she said as she slowly reached for the drawer. Her fingers felt like they belonged to someone else as she handed him the envelope. She said, "I wrote this. It's for the detective. You can give it to her when the time is right." Andy didn't take it at first. He just stared at it.

After reading the letter, he said, "You don't have to do this, mom." "Yes, I do," she replied. Andy thought for a moment and said, "You're sick. They'll just think it's a mercy confession." "Good," Marie said. He looked down. His jaw was clenched as he said, "It was me, Mama. I did it." Marie's hand found his and squeezed tight as she said, "And now it's me. That's how we make it right." Andy looked at her, his heart was breaking into quiet pieces. "But it's not right," he said. "No," she said, "It is right, and this is how it should be done." She rested her head back against the wall and said, "Andy...listen to me, baby. I don't care what people say. I know who you are. I've seen you fight through hell and still carry kindness in your heart. That night didn't make you a killer. It made you free. You have to trust me on this." He nodded once, barely. "I just want you to live now," she whispered, "I don't want you to have to hide or flinch every time someone knocks on a door." "Okay. I trust you," he said. Marie smiled, with her eyes fluttering shut. She said, "That's all I want."

CHAPTER 10

Circling the Flame

Detective Melinda Graves stood in the doorway of the shelter's common area, one hand resting inside her coat pocket where her badge sat clipped, and untouched. She didn't flash it this time. Everyone here already knew who she was. Andy was seated on the worn leather couch near the corner with a notebook on his lap. His pencil was frozen mid-sketch. He saw her the moment she entered. His eyes lifted, but his expression didn't change. "Hey, Andy," she said calmly, stepping in, "Mind if I talk to you a minute?" He closed his notebook slowly and set the pencil on top. "What now?" he asked. Before she could respond, Marie emerged from the hallway behind them. Her presence felt like a shield, frail but firm. She didn't raise her voice, but every word landed with precision. "No more questions without me present," she demanded. Graves stopped mid-step. She looked at Marie carefully. Her sunken cheeks and the dull pallor of her skin portrayed more than exhaustion. She looked like someone who was losing ground, physically and emotionally, but still refused to retreat. "I just want to clarify a few things," Graves said, "That's all." "You've clarified enough," Marie replied, crossing her arms, "He's a minor. If you have questions, they go through me." Andy looked between them but said nothing. Graves sighed, "Alright. Maybe you can clarify something then." She pulled a small folder from her satchel and opened it slowly. From inside, she removed a photo and held it up, not to Andy, but to Marie. It was the tread imprint of a shoe. Deep, narrow, and distinct. Marked by dirt and pressure. "This is the shoe print found on the front door of

Randy's house. We believe it was made when the killer kicked the door to stage a forced entry." Marie said nothing. Graves continued, "It's a size eleven. Narrow fit. Unusual for an adult male. More common in adolescents still growing into their frame." Andy shifted slightly on the couch. "We're trying to match it," Graves said, with her eyes locked on him now, "We want to compare it to shoes worn by people who were close to Randy." She continued, "Can I take a look at Andy's shoes?" Marie glanced over at Andy's feet and said, "Sure, there they are…on his feet." Andy stayed silent. Graves paused for a moment, then nodded and said, "What size shoe do you wear?" "Nine," Andy replied. "Okay," she said as she slowly tucked the photo away. She turned toward the exit but paused again, "One more thing," she said, "Motive. Everyone wants to talk about Randy's girlfriends, his drinking, and his fights, but no one had reason to want him dead like you two did. Years of abuse. No justice. No protection. Just survival." Marie stepped forward, "So, charge us. Or leave." "I can't charge you yet," Graves admitted, "Not yet." She looked at Andy one last time as she said, "But I'm close." Then she walked out. Andy had a lump in his throat he couldn't swallow down as he stared at Marie with near panic on his face.

Graves didn't go back to the precinct. Instead, she made her way across town to the East Haven Youth Outreach Center. The small brick building blended into its surroundings. It was worn and unassuming. Inside, the after-school program was in full swing. A few teens played cards in the corner. Two others practiced poetry for a school event. And near the back, alone with a book, sat Eric. Graves had heard about him at the shelter. He was another shelter kid, quiet and smart. He had trouble keeping steady attendance at school due to frequent relocations, but he had no criminal record. There were no red flags. She heard that he and Andy had spent some time together over the past few weeks, so she wanted to question him.

She approached slowly and crouched down beside his table. She said, "Eric, right?" He nodded, warily. She continued, "I'm Detective Graves. I just want to talk to you for a moment. About Andy from the shelter." Eric looked around, unsure if he was allowed to. "Is he in trouble?" he asked. "I'm trying to figure that out," she said. He looked down at the book in his hands but didn't close it. "You two are friends, right?" Graves asked. Eric shrugged, "We've stayed in the same shelter for a little while." "Do y'all talk much?" Graves asked. "Sometimes," Eric said. Graves continued, "What do you talk about?" Eric hesitated before saying, "His drawings. Mostly...maps. He likes drawing houses and escape routes." "Escape from what?" asked Graves. Eric shrugged again, "He didn't say, but you could guess." Graves nodded, "Does he ever talk about a man named Randy? His stepfather?" Eric's expression changed slightly. "Not much really. I only remember one time," he said. "What did he say?" she pressed. Eric's voice dropped, "He said some people deserve everything that happens to them." Graves watched him closely as she asked, "Did you believe him? What do you think he meant by that?" "I think," Eric said slowly, "he was trying to believe it himself." She sat down across from him now. She said, "Eric, I'm investigating a murder. I'm not looking to get anyone locked up for no reason. I just want the truth." Eric finally looked up, and there was a painful look in his eyes. He said, "He carries everything like it's his responsibility. Even the stuff that isn't. We are just kids. Kids shouldn't have to feel that way." Graves wrote the quote down. Not because it was damning. But because it was revealing. She handed him her card and said, "If you think of anything that might be important, anything at all, please call me."

She stood, thanked him quietly, and left the center. Her instincts were telling her Eric knows more than he was willing to tell. She knew this wasn't the last conversation she would have with him.

Back in her car, she reviewed her notes: Motive: crystal clear, Opportunity: strong, Circumstantial evidence: mounting. But without the weapon, without prints, without a witness or a confession, all she had was shadows and assumptions and nothing more. Marie was shielding Andy with everything she had left, but Graves could see the crack forming. She saw it in Andy's eyes. She heard it in Marie's voice. She would continue to turn up the heat. She was circling the flame. It was only a matter of time before one of them gave. And when they did, the reckoning would no longer be quiet.

CHAPTER 11

The Breaking Point

Andy had always known how to keep quiet. It was a skill he learned early on when slammed doors and clenched fists taught him the value of silence. Keep your voice low, your head down, and your thoughts to yourself. Be invisible, and you'll stay safe. He remembered the spider in the corner of the ceiling in his old room. But now, the silence was splitting him open. Each day, Detective Graves pressed closer, circling like a hawk. He could feel her eyes in every hallway, even when she wasn't there. She left a presence behind, her questions were hanging in the air, and facts whispered too loud; too close. Marie was trying to shield him by taking the heat, but Andy knew something was cracking beneath her skin too. She was sick. And not just the kind of sick you sleep off or take pills for. It was the kind that changed everything. The kind that turned time into a countdown. Andy didn't need a doctor or anyone else to translate what stage 4 colon cancer meant. He'd looked it up on the library computer when Marie wasn't paying attention. Words like "metastasized" and "palliative" hit harder than any of Randy's fists ever had. And the more he thought about it, the more it twisted inside him like barbed wire. His mother was dying, and he'd made things worse. Not just with killing Randy, but with the lies. And with the weight she now carried on top of everything else. She hadn't said it out loud, but he could see it in the way she looked at him. It was like she was preparing for something. It was like she was planning something, and he already knew what it was. She was going to confess. Not because she did it, but because she loved him and wanted to protect him. Andy had imagined a hundred versions of what would happen after that night. Some versions where no one ever found the gun, some versions where Graves moved on to a dead end, and some where he disappeared into a new life, and maybe even got out of the Baton Rouge area entirely. But not this. Not his mother sacrificing herself, again. He didn't deserve it.

One evening, he sat alone in the shelter stairwell with his knees tucked to his chest, and his sketchbook forgotten beside him. The air smelled like mildew and bleach, and the concrete walls pressed in like tombstones. He'd skipped dinner that evening. The food didn't taste like anything anymore. His hands trembled when he thought about it. Not from fear of being caught, but from the sheer weight of the lie. It was no longer just what he'd done. It was what his mother was trying to carry for him. She was coughing more in her sleep now. Her coughs were harder and longer. Sometimes she didn't stop until she had to sit up, gasping, pressing a rag to her lips. He was pretty sure he'd seen blood on it once. She tried to hide it in the trash, but he'd found it.

He pressed the heels of his palms against his eyes and clenched his teeth. He couldn't do this much longer. He didn't want her to die thinking her only purpose had been to protect him from something he brought on himself. And more than that, some small voice inside him whispered something worse: *You didn't fix anything.* Randy was gone, yes, but nothing else had healed. The fear hadn't left Marie's bones. The guilt hadn't left Andy's chest. The past still hung around their necks like a noose. He didn't feel like a hero. He didn't feel like he'd won. He felt...lost.

That night, Marie fell asleep early. She was pale and quiet, her breaths were shallow, and her body curled in the bed like a question mark. Andy sat up in bed and watched her chest rise and fall. He reached under the cot and pulled out his sketchbook. The pages were filled with maps, imaginary neighborhoods, tunnels, and escape plans. But he wasn't drawing in it anymore. Not tonight anyway. Instead, he flipped to a blank page and began to write:

Detective Graves,

I did it. Not my mom. Me.

He stopped suddenly. The pencil hovered over the page like it didn't know where to go next. What would happen after he turned it in? Would they arrest him on the spot? Would they let Marie go? Would she hate him for it? No. She wouldn't hate him. She'd be broken. Andy stared at the note for a long time. The confession half-born, scrawled in chicken-scratch handwriting. Then he slowly tore it from the notebook, crumpled it into a tight ball, and shoved it deep into the pocket of his jeans. He wasn't ready yet, but he was getting closer. And maybe, when the time came, he'd have the strength to do what needed to be done. Not to escape. Not to win. But to stop running. To finally speak. To finally tell the truth, and not just to the detective, but to himself.

CHAPTER 12

Eric's Defiance

Detective Graves wanted to have another conversation with Eric, but this time in the controlled environment of station. The stale hum of the overhead light buzzed louder than it should have, flickering faintly above the cold narrow interrogation room. Eric's mother, a stand-offish heavy-set woman, accompanied him to the station. Eric slouched in the metal chair with his arms crossed and his jaw clenched tight enough to cut nails. He looked smaller than Graves remembered. He looked like a kid trapped in the wrong part of a grown-up's world. That seemed to be the case with many boys living the shelter life.

Detective Graves stood across from him, leaning forward with both palms pressed flat on the table. Her expression wasn't angry, but it was close. It was a controlled heat. The kind that simmered under pressure. Her eyes never left his. "Tell me again," she said in a low and sharp voice, "how Andy was acting after that night." Eric exhaled through his nose and looked away but said nothing. Graves straightened slowly and began to pace the room; the heels of her boots were tapping a cold rhythm against the tile. "You're not in trouble yet. But if I find out you're hiding something, obstructing an investigation into a homicide? You'll be neck-deep in this faster than you can blink." Still, Eric didn't speak. She stopped pacing and said, "You know what I think? I think you know exactly what happened to Randy Guillaume." Eric looked up at her with a flat expression, "I already told you what I know." Graves said, "You told me Andy was upset about how Randy treated him and his mother. But you left out a few

42

things. Like the fact that he told you what he planned to do that night." Eric shifted in his seat and said, "I told you everything I know. That's all I can say about it." Graves cocked her head, "Everything? After you both spent a week talking and planning together? After you spent every spare minute whispering in corners?" She leaned in again and said, "You're protecting him." Eric's eyes flickered with a flash of uncertainty beneath the defiance. "I don't know what happened to Randy," he said in a much firmer tone this time.

Graves pulled a manila folder from the seat beside her and slid it onto the table. She flipped it open, revealing crime scene photos: Randy Guillaume's body slumped near his pickup truck in the gravel driveway with blood pooled beneath him. Eric winced as he looked away. "You know what else we found?" she continued, "A shoe print on the front door. Size 11." She walked around the table and stopped behind him. "What size shoe do you wear, Eric?" He didn't answer. Graves stepped closer. She asked, "Do you really think Andy can carry the weight of this forever? You think shielding him will help him in the long run? This isn't a playground fight. This is murder." Eric stiffened his jaw and said, "I didn't kill anybody." "I didn't say you did," Graves said, circling back to face him, "But I think you know who did. And you know where the gun came from and where it is now."

He sat still, breathing through his nose, refusing to look her in the eye. Graves took a seat across from him and folded her hands, watching him like a hawk might study a mouse that hadn't quite figured out it was already caught. "Look. I get it," she said with her voice softening just enough to sound almost human. "Randy was a piece of work. I've read the files and heard the stories. But someone still put a bullet in him, and that matters. No one deserves to die like that." Eric's lips twitched, as if he wanted to say something but was holding it back with everything he had. "Andy was scared of him," she said quietly. "I know he was. Marie and Andy left for a reason." Eric's hands clenched into fists on the table so hard his knuckles turned white. "You think he's safe now?" she asked with her voice sharpening again. "If he did it, he had no choice," Eric snapped before he could stop himself. Graves's eyes narrowed, "So he did do it." Eric cursed under his breath and slammed a hand on the table as he shouted, "I didn't say that!" "You said enough," Graves replied, unfazed. "Tell me where he got the gun. Tell me where the gun is now." There was complete silence. "Eric," she said more urgently, "if you tell me where the gun is now, that could make all the difference for Andy. It might help us understand more about what happened." Eric shook his head slowly and said, "Even if I knew, I wouldn't say. Not to you." She leaned forward again, "You're willing to let him go down for this? You want to be charged with obstruction?" "I'm willing," Eric said, making eye contact for the first time, "to not be the reason he gets charged with anything."

Graves studied him. The boy in front of her was barely fifteen, but his spine had hardened under pressure like steel. She didn't like it, but she respected it. "You're not doing him any favors," she said. Eric leaned back. His expression was resolute. "That's not for you to decide," he said. A tense silence fell over the room. Graves stood and gathered her file without another word. At the door, she paused and looked back. She said, "When the truth comes out, and it will, he's going to wish he had someone who helped him come clean instead of helping him run." Eric didn't respond. He just looked down at his hands. The door shut behind her with a heavy metallic click, leaving him alone in the humming silence. He pressed his palms to the table, steadying himself. His throat was dry, and his pulse was a steady drumbeat in his ears. But still, he had said nothing that mattered. And that, for now, was enough.

CHAPTER 13

More Pressure

Detective Graves didn't knock this time. She entered the shelter with a purpose that made the front desk volunteer rise halfway out of her seat. The young woman opened her mouth to speak, but Graves held up her badge and nodded once. "I need to speak to Marie Guillaume and Andy Collins. Now!" She demanded. The volunteer hesitated before saying, "They're in the common room…" "I'll find them," Graves said. She moved down the familiar hallway with her boots echoing in the narrow corridor. The fluorescent lights buzzed overhead, flickering faintly. The shelter always had that hum about it. It was like the whole place was on the edge of something breaking down. She found them exactly where she expected: Marie slumped on the faded couch, a wool blanket wrapped around her thin frame, and Andy beside her, quiet as ever, watching something indistinct on the muted TV screen.

When Graves entered, Marie sat up with visible effort. Andy didn't move. "No more questions," Marie said with a hoarse voice. "You made that clear. I'm not here for questions," Graves replied evenly. Marie's eyes narrowed, "Then what?" Graves removed a folded piece of paper from her coat and placed it on the table in front of them. Marie looked at it but didn't touch it. "What's that?" she asked. "An official notice from the district attorney's office," Graves said. "They've reviewed the preliminary evidence and approved a sealed juvenile case file. If my case becomes strong enough, Andy will be arrested, formally, pending further investigation." Andy's head turned slowly. His eyes met Graves's, but he didn't flinch. "You're charging him?" Marie snapped, "Based on what? A footprint that's bigger than his?" Graves remained calm, "Not yet. But I need you both to understand we're no longer in the gentle stages of this investigation. I've tried to be fair. I've tried to be patient. But there's a threshold. And we're approaching it." Marie pressed a fist to her lips. Her eyes glistened, not with fear, but with rage and desperation. "You have nothing that says he did anything," Marie said. "Not yet," Graves echoed, "But we've submitted a court order requesting a warrant for Andy's belongings, including his shoes. If any of them match the print, that's one more piece. Enough to start the formal process." "That's insane," Marie said, "You're harassing a child. A child who's been through hell." Graves looked at Andy again, and her voice softened, just slightly, "I know. I really do. But that doesn't mean there isn't truth buried in what happened. And I think it's buried inside him." She paused then said, "I also think he wants to say something." Marie looked at Andy sharply. "Don't say anything," she said. Andy didn't blink, but something flashed across his face. It wasn't fear or guilt. It was resolve.

Graves turned back to Marie and said, "You've been strong for a long time, Marie. And I respect the hell out of that. But if you're planning something, you should know: We'll find out. And when we do, it will destroy whatever credibility you have left." Marie looked down. "I'm not here to punish either of you," Graves continued. "But I am here to protect the truth. And I think, deep down, you want the same thing." Marie's shoulders sagged as she leaned back onto the couch. The blanket slipped from her lap. Her hand found Andy's without looking. "You're wanting him to confess to something he didn't do," she said quietly. Graves hesitated then said, "I want the truth." Marie didn't speak for a long time. Graves reached into her pocket again and placed a small card on the table. "That's the name of a juvenile defense attorney. A good one. Off the record. No pressure. But if things move quickly, you'll want someone in your corner." She turned to leave but she paused at the doorway. "You're running out of time," she said softly. Then she was gone.

That night, the silence in their room felt unbearable. Marie lay on her side, facing the wall. Andy sat on the edge of his cot, holding the crumpled confession note in his palm like it was burning him. He hadn't given it to Graves, but now it wasn't a question of if. It was when. Marie's breathing was labored again. That wet cough was back. He wanted to get up, bring her water, or something, but his legs wouldn't move. All he could think about was that sealed file Graves mentioned. The quiet sound of the paper hitting the table. The inevitability it carried. They were out of moves. And no matter what his mother did, no matter how much she tried to absorb the impact, the truth was coming. Andy reached down, tore the note in half, then into quarters, then into smaller pieces, letting them fall like ash to the floor. The truth didn't belong on paper. It belonged to him. And when he finally spoke it, there'd be no hiding behind letters. There'd be no shelter to run to. There'd only be the reckoning.

CHAPTER 14

Crossing Paths

The sun had barely risen when Marie removed the envelope from the drawer beside her cot. Inside the envelope was the letter she'd written to Detective Graves days earlier. Her hands trembled as she looked at the envelope. She hadn't sealed it yet. Not because she doubted the words inside, but because sealing it made it real, and she wasn't ready for that finality just yet. The letter was short. It was only two paragraphs, but one full confession. It said she had returned to the house that night. It described a moment of confrontation, and then the gunshot. It named no accomplice, or no witnesses. It was just her acting alone. It was a lie, of course, but it was a clean one. And it would buy Andy the only thing she had left to give him. Time.

She tucked the envelope inside her purse, then stood slowly, bracing herself on the edge of the cot. Every joint in her body ached now. Her gut was twisted and bloated in the mornings. The nausea never fully left her anymore. The painkillers numbed the worst of it, but they dulled her mind too. They made her feel like a ghost floating inside her own skin. Marie glanced at Andy. He was still sleeping. His face was half-buried in the crook of his arm. He looked peaceful; too peaceful for what he carried. She walked quietly to the small mirror on the wall and stared at herself. Her skin was pale. Her cheeks were hollow. There was a storm brewing behind her eyes. "This is the last thing I can do for you," she whispered. She grabbed her coat and headed out the door. Andy woke up the same moment the door clicked shut. His eyes opened slowly, but his body snapped alert fast. Marie was gone. Her coat was missing. So were her shoes. Panic flared in his chest. He sat up too quickly and swayed slightly as the adrenaline hit him like a slap to the face. She was going to confess. His heart thudded so loudly in his ears it blocked out the morning traffic outside. He stood, staggered toward the wall for balance, then yanked on jeans and a hoodie. The letter, he thought. She would be delivering it to Graves. She was doing exactly what he'd feared. And he couldn't let her. Not after everything that had happened already.

Marie sat on a metal bench outside the police precinct, staring down at the envelope in her lap. It was so small and fragile-looking, but inside it was a bomb. A lie she hoped would explode just right, clearing a path for her son to move forward. She hadn't called ahead. She didn't want Graves to have time to prepare questions. Marie just wanted to hand it over and let the process take its course. She wasn't afraid of what would follow. She was already dying. This would just be a different kind of slow death.

Footsteps approached. Marie looked up. Andy stood across the sidewalk, breathless, and wild eyed. He'd run all the way there. His sweatshirt was damp with sweat, and his chest heaved. "What are you doing?" he asked. She tried to compose her voice, "I could ask you the same thing." Andy said, "You were going to turn yourself in." Marie looked down at the envelope and said, "You shouldn't have followed me." "I had to," he said, "Because you're not the one who needs to be doing this." "Andy…" Marie gasped. He said, "No. Don't say it. You're sick. You're dying, Mom. You can't use that to take the fall for something I did." His voice cracked on the last words. He didn't mean to say them so plainly. But once they were out, there was no stuffing them back inside. Marie's face went still. She said,

"You…you were going to tell her?" Andy nodded and said, "I was trying to. I wrote it out. I couldn't give it to her. But I was close." Tears slipped from the corners of her eyes, silent and unshaken as she said, "I didn't want this for you." "I don't want you to have to pay for what I did," he replied. "I did what I did because no one else would stop him. But it didn't make me feel better. It made me scared. Every day since. And then you started getting sick, and I just…" Marie reached out and took his hand, the envelope crushed between their palms. They didn't say anything for a long time. Then she whispered, "So what now?" Andy stared at the precinct doors. Then back at her. "I don't know. But we don't lie anymore." Marie nodded.

A car pulled into the lot. Detective Graves stepped out with a coffee cup in her hand. She spotted them immediately. Andy's pulse kicked up again like a horse at full gallop. Marie looked at him and asked, "You sure?" "No," he admitted, "But I think it's time." As Graves approached, her expression was unreadable. "You two weren't on my schedule today," she said carefully. Marie stood and said, "We have something to talk about." Andy stood beside her. He said, "Together." Graves raised an eyebrow. Then motioned toward the building. She said, "Let's go inside." As they crossed the lot, the envelope remained in Marie's hand. But she didn't offer it. Not yet. Inside, a reckoning waited. But for the first time, they walked toward it side by side.

CHAPTER 15

The Weight of Silence

The interview room reeked of cold coffee and the smell of weak bleach. A single camera with a blinking red light was mounted in the corner. The overhead lights were dim with a constant hum over the heavy silence. Detective Graves sat across from Andy and Marie. Her notepad was untouched; her pen was resting between her fingers like it had been waiting a long time for this moment. Andy sat upright in the metal chair with his palms flat against his thighs. His legs were trembling, but his face held steady. He'd rehearsed every word in his head, but now, sitting here across from Graves, all the words balled up in his throat like dry bread. Marie sat beside him with both hands folded neatly in her lap. Her coat was still zipped to her neck. Her lips were pressed together tightly, but her eyes...her eyes didn't waver.

Graves broke the silence first. She said, "I appreciate you both coming. You said you had something to tell me?" Andy opened his mouth. Marie touched his arm gently. He looked at her. She looked back. And he knew. Before he said anything, before the first syllable could leave his tongue, he saw it in her face. The decision has already been made. It was irreversible and final. "I did it," Marie said suddenly. Her voice was firm but calm. "I killed Randy," she said. Graves didn't react immediately. She looked between them with her eyes narrowing slightly. Then she said, "Marie..." "I went back that night," Marie continued, "After dark. We argued. He got violent like always. He had the gun in the house. It was in the nightstand by the bed. I grabbed it while we were arguing. He dared me to shoot him. I ran out of the house. He followed me into the yard. He was saying I didn't have the guts to shoot him. Then he grabbed me and the gun went off. It was self-defense, but I panicked. I staged it to look like a robbery." Andy's mouth opened. "No!" Marie shouted. "I won't let him confess to something he didn't do," she said, as she continued raising her voice over his. Her hand was shaking now, but she didn't let go of his arm. "He was asleep. He didn't even know I was gone," she said convincingly.

Graves sat back, folding her arms. She smirked, "You're telling me you retrieved a gun, shot your husband in the chest, staged a crime scene, and returned to a shared shelter room without waking your son or being seen?" Marie nodded, "That's exactly what I'm telling you." Andy couldn't take it anymore. "She's lying," he blurted. "She's only saying this to protect me." "Andy," Marie said, turning to him with more fire than he'd seen in weeks. "Stop!" she demanded. His face crumpled. His eyes were filling with tears. He said, "Mom, you don't have to do this. I was ready. I was gonna..." "I know," she said, as her voice softened. "That's why I had to stop you."

Graves studied them both. Her expression remained unreadable, but her eyes were sharp, cataloging every detail. The emotion, the rhythm of speech, and the intent behind every word. "And where is the weapon now?" she asked finally. Marie turned back toward Graves. "I can take you to it," she said. Andy dropped his face into his hands. His chest heaved silently as he sobbed. Graves scribbled something on her pad, then looked back up. Then she asked, "Marie, you understand what this means? What you're confessing to?" Marie nodded, "I do." Andy looked at Graves through his fingers as he said, "You can't believe her. She's sick. She's dying." "I'm not dying fast enough to remain silent anymore," Marie said without looking at him. "If it were just me, I'd go to my grave with the truth. But if they come for you…if they try to put you in shackles and throw you in some detention center while I rot in a hospice bed somewhere, I wouldn't survive it. Not spiritually. Not as your mother."

Graves cleared her throat and said, "This confession will need to be verified. If we don't recover the weapon where you say it is, or if forensic evidence contradicts your story, it will not be considered credible. Do you understand?" Marie nodded again, "I'm not asking for your sympathy. Just your process." Andy wiped at his eyes and looked at Graves. "Please don't let her do this," he said. Graves's voice was quieter now, more human than cop. "Andy… I've been watching both of you for weeks. I know one of you was at that house that night. So, if your mother is giving us a confession and a murder weapon, the system won't ignore that." Marie reached into her purse and pulled out a folded piece of paper. "The directions," she said, handing it to Graves, "It's buried at the base of the oak tree directly below the big branch. There's a "V" shape where the roots enter the ground. It's wrapped in a black bandana. I can show you the exact spot if you need me to." Graves took the paper but didn't unfold it yet. She studied Marie for another long moment, then nodded slowly, "I'll send a team over there right now. If the weapon is there…well, we'll go from there." Marie nodded. Her body sagged just slightly, like she'd handed over more than a letter. Like she'd just given away what little future she had left. Graves stood and said, "You wait here." Andy stayed seated. So did Marie.

When the door finally shut behind Graves, the silence returned. Andy leaned toward her. "You didn't have to," he said. "I did," she replied. He looked away with his jaw clenched. "I hate this," he said. Marie put a hand on the side of his face and turned him toward her. "You'll grow to understand it. Maybe not forgive it but understand it," she said. He looked at her then; not as the sick, frail woman he'd been watching slowly get sicker, but as the same mother who once stood between him and Randy's rage. The same woman who had always taken the hit so he wouldn't have to. "You always save me," he whispered. Marie smiled weakly, "It's the only job I ever took seriously." Outside the room, the footsteps of officers grew louder. Inside, time began slipping away, piece by piece.

CHAPTER 16

The Trouble with Truth

Detective Graves stood in the woods behind the Everett house with her arms folded in anticipation of what was about to unearthed. The sun was angling through the trees in fractured slants. A uniformed officer kneeled beside the roots of the crooked oak tree as the crime scene technician carefully brushed away the soft earth. Another technician hovered nearby with an evidence bag, already labeled and waiting to be filled. Graves didn't need to look at the marks on the ground to know they were recent. "Got it," the tech said. He pulled a black bundle from beneath the soil, just like Marie had described. They laid it out on a clean tarp and opened it. The revolver emerged. It had a short barrel, black grip, and rust was forming at the muzzle. Graves crouched, studying it as she said, "Don't smudge the grip. Get it to the lab. Run ballistics, check for fingerprints, and run a DNA panel on the gun and the bandana." "Yes, ma'am," replied the technician.

She stood slowly with her eyes drifting toward the faint path that led back toward the Everett's fence. The woods weren't deep, but they were just wild enough to hide a secret, and just long enough for a boy to disappear and return without being noticed. Marie's confession had been tidy, but just a little too tidy. Graves was having a difficult time believing Marie's story. She claimed to have buried the gun herself, right here under the oak tree. She said she panicked, but something about it didn't sit right with Graves. The rhythm of the story didn't make sense. She opened her notebook, flipped to the page where she'd logged her earliest notes. At the top, she'd written one line in capital letters: LOOK FOR THE LIE THAT FEELS LIKE MERCY. She snapped the notebook shut.

Back at the precinct, the ballistics report was waiting: *A Single shot fired from a .38 Special. The muzzle burn indicates the shot was fired from close range. Less than one foot. No fingerprints were found.* Then the bandana. Graves sat at her desk, reading the forensics update silently. Her jaw tightened as she read: *DNA: Trace, Male, No match in CODIS.* She pushed back from her desk and stood up. She began pacing. The revolver had been wrapped in Andy's bandana she thought. That couldn't be explained away as accidental transfer. Could it? No, not if Marie had done everything herself. Then there is the shoe print. She pulled the photo again from the file. The cast was taken from the front door; size 11, narrow, worn tread. The tread design matched the style of a cheap men's sneakers. The kind that shelter volunteers sometimes handed out. She checked the timestamped list, but Andy was never issued any sneakers, at least not by the shelter.

Graves dropped into her chair and stared at the ceiling. Would a dying mother lie to protect her son? You bet she would. Because he was all she had left. She'd seen it before. She remembered another case from years back. It was an arson, a runaway teen, and a mother who claimed she'd been the one to light the match. That case had fallen apart under forensic pressure too. Mothers will lie to the world and to themselves; especially when their children are the only good thing they have left to claim. But this wasn't just about lies. It was about intent. And Graves wasn't convinced Marie had it in her to walk through a dark street, stage a fake robbery, and fire a clean shot through a man's chest. She closed the file slowly and looked out the narrow window of her office. The truth was close, but it wasn't Marie's confession that brought it near. It was everything around the confession that told her where the truth wasn't.

A knock came at her door. It was Officer Quinn. "They're bringing Marie in for formal booking," he said, "Do you want to be present for the processing?" Graves looked up and said, "No. I want to speak to Andy again." Quinn hesitated, "His mother said no more questioning without her present." Graves nodded once and said, "Then bring her back in with him. One last time." She needed to look at them together to see who blinked. To see who cracked and who held on. Because right now, Graves wasn't chasing a suspect. She was chasing a sacrifice. And she was starting to suspect the person who pulled the trigger wasn't the one holding the confession.

CHAPTER 17

A Quiet Cage

The holding room was colder than Marie expected. The chill settled in her bones, and even with her coat still on, she couldn't stop shivering. The booking process had been humiliating. Fingerprints, mugshot, and the metal detector wand sweeping over her frail frame as if she could possibly be hiding anything.

Now, she sat alone in a steel gray chair with her hands resting in her lap. Her wrists were red from the cuffs that had only just been removed. A paper cup of water sat untouched on the table in front of her. The door opened, and Detective Graves entered with Andy following behind. She had a file in her hand, and her badge was clipped visibly to her belt this time. Marie looked up, calm but unblinking. "Is this where you try to scare me into recanting my statement?" she asked Graves. Graves didn't smile. She set the folder on the table and remained standing. She told Andy to have a seat. She said, "No, Marie. This is where I try to get you to stop lying." Marie blinked slowly, then looked away. "I've seen plenty of false confessions," Graves said, "And most of them fall apart before the paperwork clears. But yours? You've clearly thought this out very carefully. The gun was right where you said it would be. The narrative's neat and tidy, but tragic." She sat down across from them. Her tone was measured, but firm. "But the evidence doesn't fit your story," she said as she glanced at Andy. Marie's voice was barely above a whisper as she said, "Why doesn't it?" Graves opened the folder. She pulled out a plastic sleeve with the photo of the shoe print taken from the front door of Randy's house. "This is definitely not your foot, Marie. I saw you walk in here. You don't weigh enough to leave a mark like this, and your foot is not nearly that big. But a teenage boy on the edge of panic might." She glared at Andy this time. Marie's face didn't move. Andy sat there silently with a blank look on his face.

Graves slid another photo across the table. It was the bandana. It was bagged and tagged. Lab results were highlighted in a printed report underneath it. Graves said, "There's DNA on the fabric, your son's. Not yours." Marie stared down at the photo but didn't touch it. She asked, "How do you know it's my son's DNA?" "I know why you're doing this," Graves continued, but softer now. "Mothers protect. It's what we do. But this…this isn't protection. It's surrender. And it won't hold." Marie finally looked up. Her voice cracked around the edges, but the words were clear, "He's just a boy." "I know," Graves replied, "The system isn't kind to boys who pull triggers. Especially if they lie about it." Marie leaned forward, as her fingers tightened around each other as she said, "He's already lost everything, his home, his peace, and his childhood. If he goes to prison, he loses the rest of his life. I won't let that happen." "And you think you can trade your own for his?" Graves asked. "You're sick, Marie. Your file says stage four. You might not even make it through a trial." Marie's breath caught in her throat, and for a moment the mask slipped. Her eyes went glassy. She said, "Then what better use is there for the time I have left?" Graves paused. It wasn't the answer she wanted, but it was the answer of a mother who'd made peace with a kind of sacrifice most people couldn't fathom. She leaned back in her chair as she said, "If you're willing to go this far for him, then tell me the whole truth. Not just the convenient version." "I've told you everything I need to," Marie said. "No, you told me what you think will keep him safe. But every piece of real evidence points to Andy. And sooner or later, the DA's going to look at that and push for a dual indictment. Especially if he thinks your confession is strategic." Marie's jaw stiffened, "You don't know what Randy was like." "I know Randy had a long history of violence," Graves said, quietly. "I know you reported bruises, and nobody followed up. I know your son watched too much, too young, and it broke something in him." Marie's voice cracked again, "It didn't break him. It made him angry. There's a difference." Graves tapped the folder once more and said, "Maybe so. But anger and intention aren't the same either. The jury will want motive. The evidence already gives them one." Marie shook her head; her eyes were swimming now. "Please don't go after him. Leave him alone," she begged. "I'm not here to play executioner," Graves said, "But I am here to find the truth. And the longer you protect him with a lie, the more danger he's in if it falls apart later." Marie's voice dropped to a whisper, "He didn't ask me to do any of this. He tried to stop me." Graves nodded. "Then let him tell me the truth." she said. Graves turned her attention toward Andy. He continued to stare blankly at the wall. Marie didn't respond immediately. After several seconds of forethought, Marie said, "The truth is in my confession."

Graves stood slowly, gathering the folder. "I'm going to give you a little time before the formal statement is locked in. You can talk to a lawyer. Think it over. But just know…if you go through with this and it doesn't hold; Andy could still face a charge. And so could you, for obstruction, making a false statement, and accessory after the fact." Marie's eyes followed her to the door. "You're a mother, aren't you?" she asked. Graves hesitated for a moment then said, "I am." Marie's voice hitched as she said, "Then you already know I won't change my mind."

Graves just stared into her eyes for several seconds and then nodded, "I do. But I'm still going to ask again tomorrow." She left the room, shutting the door behind her with a soft click. Inside, Marie and Andy sat motionless. The tremor in Marie's hands returned. Her breaths were shallow, but she forced herself to stay still. Some truths were too costly to say out loud. And some lies were simply love, wearing a braver face.

CHAPTER 18

Echoes and Pressure

Andy sat on the edge of a twin bed that didn't creak when he shifted, in a room that smelled like fresh paint instead of mildew. The shelter was behind him now. So was the cot, the cracked window, and the space he and Marie had shared for the past several weeks like a life raft barely afloat. Now he was in a small back bedroom at his Uncle Mark's house. It was like a stranger's house, really, even if Mark was family. Marie's younger brother had come for Andy after getting the call. Andy hadn't seen him in nearly four years, since a Christmas visit that ended with Marie and Mark arguing in the kitchen and Andy pretending not to hear. But when Graves asked if there was any next of kin willing to take Andy in, Mark said yes without hesitation. "I'll take care of him," he told the court-appointed caseworker, "He's family." Andy wasn't sure what that meant anymore. He stared at the floor now. His knees bounced in rhythm with the storm in his head. Marie had been gone for three days. She had been booked and processed. She was being held on charges he knew wasn't hers to bear. And it was his fault.

Across the city, Detective Graves leaned on the cool brick wall outside the school cafeteria, waiting for Eric Swann. The lunch crowd had thinned out. A counselor had arranged the meeting. "No pressure," she'd said. "Eric's not in trouble. He just might be able to help." Eric approached cautiously with his lunch tray in hand, and suspicion in his eyes. He sat across from her, watching her badge like it might bite. Graves kept her tone light, "Thanks for speaking to me again, Eric. I Just need a few more minutes of your time." He didn't speak at first. He just took a sip from the chocolate milk carton. "I have a few more questions about Andy," she said, "I know you two shared plenty of time at the shelter." Eric's shoulders lifted in a half-shrug. He said, "Not really. We played chess and we talked sometimes. That's about it." Eric was trying to distance himself from Andy as much as possible at this point. Graves nodded and asked, "The last time we spoke you said Andy never really talked much about his stepfather, right?" Eric's eyes hardened just slightly as he acknowledged, "No, he basically just said he said he was mean. And that he hurt his mom." "Did Andy ever talk about…hurting him back?" Graves asked. Eric looked away, but said, "Not really. Andy has this calmness about him. Like…when he got mad, he didn't shout. He just went inside himself. You could feel it." Graves jotted a few words in her notebook before asking, "Did he ever say anything about hiding something? The gun, maybe?" Eric hesitated, "No. But…he drew weird stuff. Like swords and knives with severed heads next to them." Graves leaned in and said, "Eric, his mom confessed. She says she did it." Eric raised both eyebrows in disbelief. He said, "No way. Miss Marie? She barely had the strength to get out of bed some days." "You don't think she could've done it?" Graves asked. Eric shook his head, "She would do anything for Andy. But that? I don't know." Graves let that settle. Then she asked, "What about Andy? Could he have done it?" Eric didn't answer right away. When he did, his voice was low, "I think he thought no one else would ever do anything to Randy." Eric glared at Graves for several seconds before asking, "Can I go now?" Graves said, "Yes, that's all I have for now, but if you think of anything Andy did or said…" She handed him her card as she continued, "Please call me. Anything at all." Eric nodded as he stood and walked away. Detective Graves was left with the same gut feeling that Eric knew more than he was saying. She had spoken with him several times now hoping he would slip up, but the kid was a very tough nut to crack.

Back at Mark's house, Andy sat at the kitchen table with blank eyes as the late afternoon sunlight poured in. Mark moved around the room, not saying much, just cleaning up dishes that didn't need cleaning and offering food Andy never touched. The man was tall, heavyset, wore old flannel, and smelled like aftershave and menthol. He wasn't unkind, just unsure. "You eat anything today?" Mark asked. Andy shook his head. "You want a grilled cheese?" Mark asked. "No, thanks," Andy replied. Mark sighed and leaned against the counter and said, "I don't know what to say to you, kid. I ain't a dad. Hell, I ain't even a good uncle. But I'm trying." Andy gave him a faint nod but kept his eyes on the table. Mark crossed his arms. He said, "Your mama…she's always been tough. Stubborn too. When she makes up her mind about something, that's it. But this? Confessing to murder?" He shook his head, "Something ain't right." Andy looked up sharply, "You think I did it?" Mark paused before saying, "I think somebody had to stop that bastard. And I think your mama would rather die than watch you get swallowed up by the system." Andy looked away again. His throat was tight.

That night, Detective Graves arrived at Mark's house unannounced. Her motherly instincts led her to check on Andy. Mark answered the door, wiping his hands on a towel. Andy peeked from the hallway. "Detective Graves, right?" Mark said, stiffly, "What can I do for you?" "Just here to talk to Andy if I may," she said. "Not official. Off the record." Mark turned back and said, "Andy? She wants to speak to you." Andy stepped forward cautiously. Graves kept her voice even, "How you holding up?" Andy just nodded. She studied his face for a moment. Then she said, "Your mom insists she acted alone." Andy's eyes didn't flinch. "But here's the thing," she continued, "The shoeprint on the door? Clearly not hers. And male DNA was on the bandana found with the gun." Mark swore softly under his breath, "DNA?" Graves nodded. She said, "I just need to know, Andy, do you want to let her take this all the way?" Andy opened his mouth, but the words got stuck. His eyes burned, but he didn't blink. He just whispered, "She made her choice." Graves studied him a moment longer, then handed Mark her card. She said, "If either of you wants to talk, you know where to find me."

After she left, Mark turned to Andy, "Is she taking responsibility for what you did?" Andy's voice broke, "I didn't ask her to." "But you're letting her," he said. Andy didn't answer. Because he didn't know how to. Mark then said, "We may need to get you an attorney before this goes any further." Andy just nodded and shrugged.

CHAPTER 19

The Weight of Evidence

District Attorney Joel Whitaker had seen a hundred confessions in his twenty-three years. Some were real. Some were manufactured. Some were half-truths meant to protect someone else. That's what this one felt like. He leaned back in his office chair, the blinds were casting gray slats of light across his desk. The case file in front of him was thick and officially titled *State of Louisiana v. Marie Celeste Guillaume*. A confession, a murder weapon, and a known history of domestic violence. On paper, it looked solid. Almost too solid. Detective Graves sat across from him with her arms folded, and a tension in her jaw that never really went away. "She's insisting she acted alone?" Whitaker asked, tapping the folder. "She hasn't wavered," Graves replied. "Claims she went back to the house that night, shot Randy, then fled. She says she buried the gun in the woods behind the neighbor's property because it felt symbolic." Whitaker frowned, "Symbolic?" Graves continued, "She said it was where Andy used to play. She said she wanted to bury what haunted him." Whitaker scoffed lightly, "Poetic, convenient, and complete bullshit." Graves smirked, but only faintly, "You think she's covering for the boy too?" "I know she is," he replied. "But knowing and proving are two different things." He opened the folder and said, "Let's walk through it again."

He flipped to the forensics summary. He said, "The gun belonged to Randy Guillaume. Ballistics confirmed it is the murder weapon. And it was recovered exactly where she said it would be." Graves nodded. "No fingerprints?" he asked. "None on the gun," she replied. "But the bandana wrapped around the gun has male trace DNA on it with no match in CODIS." "And the shoeprint at the scene?" he asked. Graves replied, "Size eleven. Doesn't exactly match Andy's shoe size, but I suspect maybe he didn't wear his own shoes. It's definitely not Marie's though. She wears women's size eight. Too small to match." Whitaker steepled his fingers and said, "So, circumstantial, and it has very little weight." Graves said, "She claims the bandana had been in Andy's backpack at some point. She says he has handled it many times. She tries to paint it all as coincidence." "Too many coincidences," Whitaker muttered. "Where was Andy that night?" he asked. Graves replied, "At the shelter. According to her." Whitaker asked, "No staff confirmation?" Graves confirmed, "Not one person saw him between 10:00 p.m. and 6:00 a.m. That's when the murder occurred. But there's no camera and no definitive alibi." Whitaker had frustration in his voice as he said, "And he hasn't admitted anything at this point?" Graves shook her head, "Not outright. But he's cracking. You can feel it."

Whitaker sighed and closed the folder. He said, "We can push forward on her. Accept her confession. It makes sense. The domestic abuse, battered woman syndrome, and mental duress." "She's sick," Graves said, more quietly. "I read the medical report," he replied, "Stage four colon cancer. Metastasis confirmed. Six months, maybe less." They sat quietly for a long time. Finally, Whitaker asked, "You really think she's using it like that?" "Maybe. I think she's at peace with dying if it means saving her kid," Graves replied. After a few more moments of silence, Graves looked up and asked, "So what do you want to do?" Whitaker tapped the folder once again and said, "We file charges. First-degree murder, unlawful possession of a firearm, and tampering with evidence. We let her sit for a while." "And Andy?"

Graves asked. Whitaker took a long pause then said, "If he cracks, he cracks. If he doesn't, we watch him. Maybe we'll never know the full story." Graves nodded slowly, but her gut twisted. She didn't like question marks in murder cases. They lingered. They infected everything. "Can I keep pressing him?" she asked. "Carefully," Whitaker warned. "She's already warned us not to speak to him alone. Legal representation may come into play soon. You push too hard, you risk suppressing what little we have." Graves stood and said, "Okay, I'll keep digging."

As she left the DA's office and stepped back into the noise of the courthouse hallway, she passed Marie in cuffs, being escorted from the holding room. Marie's skin was pale. Her eyes were sunken. Her body looked like it was collapsing in slow motion, inch by inch. Their eyes met briefly. Marie said nothing, but Graves saw the steel behind her pain. The unyielding will of a mother walking herself to slaughter. And Graves hated that she understood it.

Back in Mark's house, Andy sat at the kitchen table. He always returned to the same spot after school. He traced circles on a notepad; his stomach was a hollow echo. Mark stepped in from the living room, holding a folded letter. He said, "This came from the jail." Andy took it from him slowly. His name was written in Marie's careful, looping script. He opened it with trembling fingers.

My sweet boy,

I know this must be tearing you apart, but I need you to understand something: I have lived in fear for most of my life. Fear of being alone. Fear of being wrong. Fear of being weak, and worst of all, fear that I wouldn't be able to protect you. I won't let that be how this ends. Let them take me. I made peace with it the moment I saw your face that morning, still whole and still here. Don't undo that. Live. That's all I ever wanted for you.

Love, Mama

Andy pressed the letter to his chest. He wanted to cry, but he didn't. He wanted to scream, but he didn't. Instead, he whispered to the silence, "I didn't want this." But the silence didn't answer. And the weight stayed right where it was.

CHAPTER 20

The Turning Gears

The courtroom smelled faintly of lemon furniture polish and dust. It was too cold inside, like the chill was part of the design; meant to keep everyone alert, and on edge. Marie sat at the defense table in a beige jumpsuit; her wrists were shackled in front of her. Her body felt foreign to her now. It felt weaker. Like it was no longer hers to command.

The public defender assigned to her, Rachel Keane, was younger than Marie had expected. She appeared to be in her early thirties. She wore a sharp black blazer. Her hair was pinned and rested neatly at the nape of her neck. She reminded Marie of a social worker from a lifetime ago, one who had once offered help before the doors closed behind her again. "First-degree murder, tampering with evidence, and illegal possession of a firearm," Rachel whispered, leaning over. "They're not offering any deal yet. They want to push this." Marie nodded once, "That's fine." Rachel studied her for a moment and said, "They're going to say you're exploiting your illness to save your son. That you're unstable." "I'm not unstable," Marie said with a raised voice. Loud enough to make heads turn in the courtroom. "I don't think you are," Rachel whispered. Marie hesitated, then said, "I did it. By myself. I just...couldn't take it anymore." Rachel nodded, scribbling a note as she asked, "And the gun?" Marie said, "I knew where he kept it." "Did your son know?" asked Rachel. Marie's eyes flicked toward her hands as she said, "No, he didn't." Rachel let the silence stretch. Then she said, "They're looking at him you know. They have a shoe print and male DNA on the bandana.

They have requested a court order to do a DNA swab on him." Marie's voice was sharp, "He didn't do it." Rachel didn't argue. She said, "We'll do everything we can. But you need to prepare yourself. If the evidence keeps pointing to him, they may try to undermine your confession." Marie growled, "I won't let them touch him."

The judge entered the courtroom, and everyone stood as the Bailiff said, "All rise." The arraignment was brief. Marie's plea was entered. Bail was denied. A trial date was scheduled. When Marie was led back to holding, she didn't glance at the gallery. There was no one there for her. She walked back to the holding cell alone.

Meanwhile, in a quiet house across town, Andy sat at the dining room table, staring at the letter again. His uncle Mark had gone to work, leaving him alone for the afternoon. The house was quiet except for the distant ticking of the wall clock and the soft hum of the dishwasher. The silence felt like judgment. He'd read Marie's letter four times already. He'd memorized it. Her words wrapped around him like a blanket soaked in guilt. He rose and paced the room, stopping at the window. The street looked the same as it always had. Cars were passing. Dogs were barking behind chain-link fences. A group of kids were kicking a flat soccer ball up the sidewalk. How could the world look normal when everything inside him was crumbling? He pressed his forehead against the palm of his hand. His chest felt too tight. His right hand wouldn't stop twitching. He remembered the weight of the gun in his palm. The finality of the trigger. The way Randy's body had dropped. He hadn't expected it to be that fast or that quiet. Andy squeezed his eyes shut. He hadn't done it out of hate; not really. He'd done it because it felt like there was no other choice. It was like the world was collapsing and he could either hold the door or be crushed by it. And now, Marie was behind bars for it. She was dying, and she'd chosen to spend the time she had left shielding him from the worst consequences of what he'd done. He felt he didn't deserve that.

He reached for his backpack and pulled out his notebook. There were lots of pages of sketches. Sketches of old maps and scribbled lines of thoughts that never quite formed full sentences. On the last page, he wrote a single question with a shaky pen: *What kind of person lets someone else die for their mistake?* He stared at the words, willing them to offer an answer, but they didn't.

Just then, the front door creaked open. Andy jumped, slamming the notebook shut and quickly putting it back in his backpack. Mark stepped in, carrying a brown bag of groceries. "Hey kid," he said, setting the bag on the counter, "Picked up some spaghetti. You eat today?" Andy shrugged, "Not really." "You should. You're gonna need your strength," Mark said. He hesitated, then added, "I, uh, saw the news. They're charging your mom. DA's pushing for first-degree murder." Andy nodded slowly. Mark pulled out a chair and sat across from him. He said, "You know...you don't have to say anything. But I just want you to know, if you need to talk, really talk, I'll listen. I ain't gonna judge you." Andy looked at him, surprised, "Why would you say that?" Mark gave a small, sad smile, "Because I remember your mom when she was your age. She carried a weight around on her shoulders, too. Always trying to be the adult in the room. Always protecting people." Andy looked down, "She thinks she's protecting me too." Andy stood quickly causing the chair to screech on the floor. "I need some air," he said. Mark didn't stop him. Andy stepped out into the late afternoon light. The air was thick with the smell of freshly cut grass and distant rain. He didn't know where he was going, but his legs started moving toward something he wasn't ready to face but maybe needed to. Because at some point, the truth stops being a weight you carry, and starts being a debt you owe.

CHAPTER 21

Cracks in the Story

Detective Graves stared at the screen again. It was her fifth time watching Marie's confession. The video was a little grainy due to the poor lighting in the room. Marie sat across the table with her hands folded, and her voice was flat and unwavering. She'd claimed she walked the five and a half miles from the shelter to Randy's house in the middle of the night. She claimed she grabbed his gun from the nightstand. She claimed the gun went off when he grabbed her before walking calmly back, unseen, and unheard. It didn't make sense. Graves clicked pause. The problem wasn't just the story. It was how clean the scene was. No trace of Marie's presence. No footprints matching her small, worn sneakers. No surveillance footage of a woman limping down the sidewalk. No witnesses spotting her leaving or returning to the shelter. And the kicker, Marie's medical records, which Graves had finally gotten her hands on. Stage 4 colon cancer. Significant fatigue. Degenerative joint pain. The kind of condition that made climbing a single flight of stairs feel like a battle. She didn't walk that far. Not in the middle of the night. Not in the condition she was in.

Graves stood and tucked the file under her arm, then made her way to the jailhouse interview room. She had requested another meeting. Marie had agreed without protest. The guard buzzed her in. Marie sat in the same position as before, only now, her face was paler, and her eyes were ringed with exhaustion. She looked thinner than she had just days ago. The jumpsuit hung off her frame. "Detective," Marie said simply as Graves sat across from her. "Marie," Graves said in return, laying the file flat between them. Graves continued, "I wanted to go over a few things in your statement again." Marie nodded with an expression on her face that said: *Get over it, already*. Graves said, "You said you used Randy's revolver that you took from the nightstand." "That's right," Marie said. Graves opened the folder, flipping to a page while saying, "Except there's no evidence you entered the house. There were no signs of a struggle. You said there was an argument. Was that inside the house?" "Yes," Marie answered. Graves continued, "So, Randy just let you walk right over to the nightstand and grab the gun?" Marie didn't blink. She sat in silence for a moment. Then she said, "Maybe it wasn't in the nightstand, then. Maybe it was in the kitchen. I don't recall." Graves smiled faintly. "I understand memory isn't always perfect. But I also pulled your medical file." Marie's eyes glanced downward. Graves continued, "I know the side effects of your cancer. The fatigue. The pain. You can't walk more than a block without needing to stop, can you?" Marie looked up slowly. Her voice cracked slightly, "I don't want to die and leave all this on him." Graves softened, just a little. "I believe that. I believe you want to protect him. But Marie...this isn't the way." "He's a child," Marie said, firmer now. "He doesn't deserve to lose everything over something he didn't do." she said. Graves leaned forward and said, "And I would agree if that were the case. But you're asking me to close a murder case based on a story that doesn't line up. We found male trace DNA on the bandana the gun was wrapped in. I suspect it's Andy's DNA." Marie's hands tightened in her lap. Graves slid a document across the table. She said, "We've secured a court order. The judge signed off on it this morning. We'll be collecting a DNA sample from Andy within the next forty-eight hours." Marie's breath caught in her throat. Her eyes filled, but she blinked the tears away quickly. "You can still help him," Graves said softly, "But not by taking the fall. Not with lies. If we go to trial with what we have now, the inconsistencies in your story will tear your credibility apart. The prosecutor will be forced to ask why you're really confessing. If Andy gets pulled into this after your false confession…" "He won't be pulled in," Marie interrupted with a sharp tone, "Because I won't let him." "You can't control that forever," Graves said, "And if the DA thinks you're lying to cover for him? That puts him at even more risk." Marie looked down again with her jaw clenched. The sickness was eating away at her and Graves could see it. It wasn't just the disease, but the ache of knowing the truth might destroy them both. After a few minutes of silence, Marie spoke, "Have you ever loved someone more than you love life itself?" Graves hesitated, "Yes. I have." "Then you know," Marie said quietly, "You know what it is to choose them, even when it costs you everything." Graves nodded slowly and said, "I do. Which is why I'm giving you one more chance to come clean. If there's anything you want to clarify, now is the time." But Marie only leaned back in her chair, folding her arms again. She said, "I already told you everything I can." Graves stood slowly shaking her head. As she picked up the file, she said, "Okay. Then I'll be in touch." As she walked out, her expression was grim. She could feel the gears of the case shifting again. The DA was circling. The pressure was on. But she also knew something Marie hadn't counted on: Teenagers carry secrets like glass bottles. And eventually, they break.

CHAPTER 22

Echoes and Evidence

Andy sat in a small room at the jailhouse; his knees were bouncing against the edge of the stiff plastic chair. The walls were white. Not hospital white, but the kind of dull, scratched-up white that felt temporary, like nothing here was ever meant to last. Across from him, a nurse in light blue scrubs adjusted a sterile swab and sealed plastic tube. Her expression was neutral; her movements were clinical. To her, this was just a job. Just another sample from just another kid. But to Andy, it felt like the point of no return. "Just open your mouth and tilt your head back a bit," she said softly. Andy obeyed. His mouth was dry. The swab scraped along the inside of his cheek. The sensation was both insignificant and world-ending. "There we go," she said, sliding the swab into the tube and labeling it. "You're all done." Andy nodded with his eyes down as they followed the nurse out of the room.

Uncle Mark was waiting in the hallway, leaning against the wall with his arms crossed. He gave Andy a small nod but didn't speak. Neither of them had much to say. They rode in silence on the way back to Mark's house on the outskirts of town. Mark was Marie's half-brother. They shared the same mother. He was a former truck driver who'd long since traded cross-country hauls for slacks and polo shirts behind a desk. Mark didn't talk much, but he didn't judge either. And right now, that was enough. Andy sat on the edge of the spare bed, staring at the patterns in the old quilt. His mind reeled, not just from the DNA swab, but from the knowledge that no matter what Marie said, no matter how much she tried to shield him, it was all falling apart.

And then there was Eric. Andy hadn't talked to him since the first day Graves came to the shelter. Since that brief moment in the hallway when they'd exchanged a glance that said more than words ever could. He wondered what Eric had told her. He wondered what Eric would tell her. Detective Graves leaned forward slightly, watching Eric fidget in the plastic chair across from her in the station's interview room. It was the fourth time she was going to interview him. Her gut had always told her he knew more than he was telling her. Her questions were redundant, but she was hoping his story would change or he would say something different. He wore a different hoodie each time, but he wore the same nervous eyes. "You doin' okay, Eric?" Graves asked gently. He shrugged, glancing at the camera mounted in the corner of the room. "I guess," he said. "No trouble at the shelter? No pressure from anyone to say or not say anything?" she asked. "No, ma'am," he replied. Graves gave a small nod and clicked her pen. Then she said, "Eric, you told me before that Andy's been through a lot. That he keeps to himself. But I need to ask again…and I need you to think carefully this time…did he ever say anything about doing anything to Randy? Anything about what he wanted to do to Randy?" Eric hesitated. Graves waited. She let the silence stretch just long enough to make the air feel tight. Finally, Eric spoke, "He didn't say it straight out. Not like, 'I'm gonna kill him.' But…he said he wished someone would make it stop. That he was tired of waiting for someone else to do something." Graves nodded slowly, "Do you think he meant himself?" Eric swallowed hard and said, "I don't know. Maybe." Graves said, "You were the one who told him not to run. That it would make things worse. Did you two ever talk about a gun?"

Eric blinked and replied, "No." Graves continued, "Did he ever show you anything he was hiding?" Eric shook his head, "I swear, I don't know anything. I don't even know if he left that night." Graves leaned back. Her tone softened, "Eric, you're not in trouble. I just need to understand who Andy talks to, who he trusts. Was he acting strange after that night?" Eric rubbed his hands together slowly as he said, "He stopped drawing. That's how I knew something wasn't right. I wasn't sure what exactly, but it was weird. He always had his sketchpad open drawing maps. Not real ones, just...made-up places." Eric continued, "He tore them all out of his sketchpad after that night. He burned them in the barrel out back at the shelter." Graves jotted the note. "Did he say why?" she asked. Eric stared down at his hands and said, "He said he didn't need them anymore." She tapped her pen against the table in a subtle, steady rhythm. Eric looked up with troubled eyes. "Is he gonna go to jail?" he asked. "I don't know," Graves answered honestly. "That depends on a lot of things." Eric shifted in his seat as he said, "He's not a bad person. You know that, right?" "I do," Graves said, watching him, "That's why I want the truth. No matter where it leads."

Back at Mark's house, Andy stood in the backyard beneath a narrow slice of sky. The air was thick with the scent of cut grass and truck exhaust from the nearby highway. It should've felt like any other summer afternoon, but nothing felt normal anymore. He could almost hear his mother's voice in the wind. The soft rasp she had when she was tired. She'd made her choice. She'd stepped in front of the bullet meant for him, but Graves was still digging. The swab had been taken. The truth was clawing its way to the surface.

Andy took a deep breath and stared up at the sky. His hands were in his pockets, clenched into fists so tight his nails left marks in his skin. He wanted to run. Not away, but toward something. Toward truth. Toward freedom. But even now, with everything closing in, part of him still didn't know how. Inside, Mark's voice called through the back door, "Dinner." Andy turned and walked slowly toward the house. He didn't know what tomorrow would bring. But he knew it was coming fast.

CHAPTER 23

Thresholds

District Attorney Joel Whitaker sat at the long glass conference table in his corner office, a stack of manila folders spread out like an unfinished puzzle. Outside the tall windows, the Baton Rouge sky simmered in the late afternoon haze. Inside, the air was crisp with recycled AC and the faint scent of strong coffee. It was his third cup today, but it sat untouched and was getting cold.

Detective Melinda Graves stood across from him. Her arms were crossed, but her posture was respectful. She didn't pace or fidget. Graves knew how to wait. She knew this part mattered. Whitaker flipped through the pages of the forensic report again with his eyes narrowing on the highlighted paragraph near the bottom: *Trace amounts of touch DNA consistent with juvenile male identified as Anthony Collins were recovered from the black bandana that was recovered with the firearm. However, no direct skin cell contact on the weapon itself was found.* Whitaker tapped the page and said, "So the kid's DNA is on the bandana, but nowhere else?" Graves nodded in agreement and said, "Correct. And he'd used that bandana before. The mother says it was part of his belongings. We don't have proof he touched it the night of the murder." Whitaker's brow tightened. He said, "But the weapon was buried. That's deliberate concealment." "Yes," Graves said. "But Marie led us to it. She claimed full responsibility. She said she acted alone. And she told a story that, on its face, fits. That she took the weapon and hid it herself." Whitaker sighed, leaning back in his chair, "Her story is a little too neat. If Marie's lying to protect him, we have to prove it. Otherwise, it's her confession versus weak forensics." "Exactly," Graves said.

Whitaker let the silence settle. He didn't rush his conclusions, especially not when the stakes were this high. A 13-year-old suspected of murder. A mother who'd thrown herself on the legal grenade. Public perception. Political pressure. Ethics. All of it will be coiled together like live wires. "Let's break this down," Whitaker said finally, "What do we know?" Graves pulled a fresh page from her folder and slid it across the table. She said, "The timeline is tight. Randy Guillaume was shot sometime between 1:30 and 5:15 a.m. That's based on body temperature and the neighbor's statement. According to Marie, Andy was asleep in the shelter. The night staff has confirmed they saw Andy at curfew and again before breakfast. But no one can say for sure where he was between ten and four in the morning." Whitaker nodded slowly, "All circumstantial." Graves said, "The DNA on the bandana…maybe not enough alone, but it leans his direction." "But leans isn't enough," Whitaker muttered, "We're not in the business of guesses. We have to prove it beyond a reasonable doubt. And right now, we can't." He leaned forward again, his hands steepled, "If we charge the boy and the confession sticks, we risk a suppression hearing that blows the whole case. We also risk looking like we're ignoring a clear confession from a dying woman. Public defenders love that angle. And if she dies before trial…" "She's already stage four," Graves added grimly, "Clock's ticking."

Whitaker stared out the window for a moment. Then he said, "What about Eric? The boy Andy's close with from the shelter. Any new leads there?" Graves said, "He confirmed Andy burned his drawings after the murder. He said Andy had talked about wishing someone would stop Randy. But nothing concrete.

Nothing like a confession." Whitaker reached for his coffee, took a sip, and grimaced. It was cold. He set it back down. "Here's what I want," he said. "I want you to keep the pressure on. Press Marie harder but try to use some compassion. Push the uncle for anything he might know. Re-interview Eric if we have to. If Marie is lying, she'll slip up soon. And if Andy's going to come forward, he'll do it under pressure, not in a courtroom." Graves nodded and said, "Understood." Whitaker stood, picking up the folder and tapping the edge on the desk as he said, "This is a powder keg, Melinda. A worried kid. A battered mother. A dead man that nobody mourns. But that doesn't mean we shortcut justice." Graves looked him in the eye, "I don't intend to." "Good. Then we do what we always do," Whitaker said as he turned toward the window, "We wait for the crack."

Back at Mark's house, Andy sat at the kitchen table, a bowl of uneaten cereal growing soggy in front of him. Mark moved around in the small kitchen behind him, cleaning up from breakfast in his quiet, efficient way. A letter sat on the table between them. It was from the DA's office. Andy hadn't opened it. Mark set down the sponge and dried his hands. "You want me to read it?" he asked. Andy shook his head and said, "Not yet." Mark nodded and sat across from him. "Whatever happens, kid, you're not alone," he said. Andy looked up with hollow eyes and said, "She's going to die thinking this was the only way." Mark sighed, "She's trying to protect you. That's what she thinks matters." Andy stared at the letter and said, "But I didn't protect her." He pushed the bowl away. The silence between them was the kind that didn't ask for answers. Just the truth. And it was coming, whether they were ready or not.

CHAPTER 24

The Line Between

Detective Melinda Graves sat at her desk well past sundown, the hum of the precinct dimming as other detectives clocked out and the day shift rolled into night. The overhead fluorescents buzzed above her, echoing the static hum in her mind. Her desk was covered in papers, photos, and the case file she knew better than her own birthday by now: Randy Guillaume. Deceased. Single gunshot wound to the chest. One confessed killer. One boy with everything to lose. She rubbed her eyes and leaned back in her chair, staring at the ceiling like it might offer a different answer than the one her gut had been fighting for weeks.

The forensic report lay open in front of her with the words burned into her thoughts by now: *Trace DNA recovered on exterior of bandana consistent with Anthony Collins. No direct contact with firearm.* She turned the page again, even though she didn't need to. The shoeprint analysis. A large, narrow treaded sneaker print on the kicked-in front door. Two sizes bigger than Andy's; not definitively his. But Graves thought all along he might have been wearing borrowed sneakers at the time of the murder. There is no proof of her theory. No eyewitness. No surveillance footage. No digital footprint. Just a mother's confession, a buried weapon, and a boy whose silence screamed guilt, but didn't prove it.

Graves stood and walked to the whiteboard on the far wall. Randy's name was circled at the top, with the timelines and photos stretching out like spider legs from the center. Beneath it, Marie's name. Then Andy's. Below that, one word she'd written weeks ago and hadn't erased: *Motive*. She picked up the dry erase marker and hovered over the board, as if another theory might suddenly surface. Marie was dying. That was a fact. Her doctor said six months, maybe less. She could have seen the writing on the wall, made peace with whatever judgment she'd face in this life or the next, and decided her son deserved a life she never had. Freedom, safety, and a second chance. But something in it still felt…wrong. Graves had seen plenty of mothers lie for their kids. But this lie…this calculated, methodical confession…was one of the cleanest she'd ever come across. Too clean. So clean, it was brittle. Still, the law wasn't built on instinct. It was built on evidence. And theirs was razor thin.

The phone on her desk buzzed. Graves turned and answered, "Graves." "DA Whitaker," came the voice, "I read your last summary. Sounds like we're cornered." Graves hesitated then said, "I hate it, but…yes." "Without a confession from Andy, without a witness or hard forensics, we've got nothing solid. The bandana DNA can be explained in a dozen ways. The shoe print isn't a match. The murder weapon was obviously handled with gloves. There's no direct tie to Andy except for things that could be chalked up to proximity or past use. Marie's confession holds up better than it should." "I know," Graves said. "But she's lying. I'm sure of it." "I don't doubt that," Whitaker replied. "But being sure and proving it in court are two different mountains. We push Andy now, and we look like we're targeting a kid with no priors while ignoring a signed confession from a terminal woman who led us to the gun. That's a PR disaster. And a legal one." Graves said nothing. "We may have to let it stand," Whitaker continued. "Charge Marie formally and file under special circumstances, given her condition. At this point, that's our best shot at closure." Graves clenched her jaw and said, "She's going to die in custody."

"I know," said Whitaker. Graves said, "I don't want to bury the real truth with her." "And I don't want to walk into court with a case that collapses in front of a jury," Whitaker said, sharp but fair. "You want to keep digging, be my guest. But we can't hold this over the boy's head forever. At some point, we have to move forward." Graves ended the call and stared at her desk. The truth didn't care how she felt. It didn't matter how much she believed in her gut that Andy had pulled the trigger. The truth wasn't a hunch, it was evidence, and the burden of proof was merciless. In the courtroom, feelings don't matter. Only facts do. And the facts, as they stood, pointed to a dying woman's final act of sacrifice. Graves sat down again and slowly closed the file.

Across town, Marie lay curled on a thin mattress in the jail infirmary, coughing into her pillow, her body was weakening day by day. And miles away, Andy sat at Mark's kitchen table, doing his best to finish his homework as the news whispered updates in the background. His fingers tapped the table with a quiet, nervous rhythm. The pressure was still there, but something had changed. The storm hadn't passed, but it had stalled. Detective Graves had walked to the edge of the line. And, for now, she hadn't crossed it. But that line wasn't gone. It was just waiting. And she was still watching.

CHAPTER 25

The Fray at the Edge

Detective Melinda Graves didn't expect much from the property clerk's message. A box of Randy Guillaume's personal effects had finally cleared the backup at central evidence. A box of leftover contents from the glove box and truck bed that weren't logged into the primary file. She almost didn't bother picking it up herself. But habit had always been her compass. And habit said you turn over every rock.

The box sat on a dented metal table in the evidence intake room, marked "secondary non-critical; Guillaume homicide." Graves opened the lid with a sigh and shuffled through the contents: a few grimy receipts, a rusted tire gauge, and a scratched-up metal flashlight. Then her hand landed on a disposable camera. She froze. It was a generic model. The kind sold at gas stations with 24 exposures. It was wrapped in faded plastic and dusted with grime. Graves turned it over. The frame counter read "4." Only four photos had been taken. She walked it straight to evidence imaging. "Can we rush this?" she asked. The tech, a lanky man with thick glasses, looked it over. He said, "Film's old, but appears in good shape. I'll see what I can get." Graves nodded and left him to it. The wait was short.

Thirty minutes later, he returned with a small stack of printed photos and a flash drive. "You might want to look at these," he said. Graves spread the prints on the desk. The first three showed nothing out of the ordinary. Just two blurry shots of an engine block, probably from some repair Randy had been working on, and one of the front porch at night, just a sliver of light catching the truck. But the fourth image made her sit up straighter. It was Randy, seated on a lawn chair near the truck, beer in hand, clearly unaware the photo was being taken. He was mid-gesture, his mouth was slightly open, as if he was speaking. Behind him, barely visible in the deep shadow, was a human figure. Graves squinted. The person appeared young and lean. Mostly obscured by darkness, but not entirely. The angle didn't show a face. But the shape, the posture, and the height…and the detail that clenched her stomach, the bandana. It was black and tied low around the figure's neck. Graves sucked in a slow deep breath. It wasn't proof. It wasn't a smoking gun. But it was something. Something new. Something that put a figure matching Andy's build in a photo with Randy and wearing a black bandana around his neck. A moment preserved unknowingly and forgotten until now. It's unknown when the picture was taken, but maybe forensics can analyze it and get more detail. Graves shoved the prints into a folder and rushed out of the room.

At the jail infirmary, Marie's latest bloodwork had triggered an automatic transfer from general population to the medical ward. The cancer was no longer manageable since it had spread to her liver. The nurses had whispered it was only a matter of time. Marie could feel it. Her limbs ached constantly. Her appetite was gone. Some mornings, she woke up unsure whether it was dawn or dusk. The world blurred at the edges, as though her body was trying to leave before she had. Still, she clung to the one thing that mattered. Andy. She'd asked her public defender to check on him again, just to see how he was doing. She hadn't heard anything since the court ordered his DNA collection. The guard said he was still with Mark, but that didn't calm the dull ache behind her ribs. She missed him. She missed the way he curled into his hoodie when he was nervous. She missed the sound of him pacing the room when he thought she was asleep. She had done what she had to. There was no regret in that. Her only worry was that it hadn't been enough.

Graves sat in her office, the image from the camera blown up on her screen. She'd enhanced the contrast, sharpened the shadow lines. She could make out a little more now, the slope of the shoulder, the angle of the legs. It was definitely a teenaged boy. She'd staked enough surveillance to know the difference. And it was Andy. It had to be. But the photo wasn't clear enough to present in court as identification. No face, no forensic tie. No timestamp authentication from a digital source. The defense would rip it apart. She tapped her pen against her notebook. "Who took the picture?" Randy was clearly unaware it had been snapped. Was it accidental? Timed? A joke gone wrong? Or…something else? She glanced again at the corner of the photo. In the dark shadow behind Randy and the boy, another object sat in the grass, half-lost in blur and shadow. She zoomed in. It took her a minute. It looked like a small case of some sort. It was small, soft and open.

Graves flipped open the original case contents list. No small soft case had been logged. The case was insignificant at best. But if someone else had borrowed the camera, used it, or handled it…there might be prints on the body of it. Maybe even Andy's. It wasn't much. But it was another thread. And when the case frays at the edge, threads are all you've got. She picked up the phone and dialed for forensics. "Hey, I need prints run on the disposable camera body. Yes, again. Everything you can lift. And I want cross-reference runs against both Marie Guillaume and Anthony Collins." She hung up and looked back at the photo. The silence in the image haunted her. Like a moment caught just before the truth exploded. Something still didn't sit right. A mother's lie carried weight, but it also carried cracks. And Andy? The boy was unraveling from the inside out. She could feel it. They were close to the truth. So close, the lie couldn't hold much longer. She just had to be patient. The bandana. The photo. The prints. The cancer. And one family clinging to a secret Graves wasn't ready to bury: at least not yet.

CHAPTER 26

Let It Go

The air conditioning vent above Graves' desk whispered like a warning as she stared at the forensic report on her screen. The results from the disposable camera had come back earlier that morning. She'd known they were long shots. A Hail Mary tossed from the shadow of doubt, but she'd clung to hope anyway.

There were no usable fingerprints on the plastic shell. The surface had degraded over time. Partial prints were smudged beyond viability. There was nothing definitive. And nothing linking Andy to the camera itself. As for the photo, the enhancement algorithms had done what they could, but even at maximum resolution, the figure remained a blur in the dark. A boy, yes. Hooded, narrow-shouldered, and likely under 5'8", but no clear facial markers. No time stamp that would hold up in court. Nothing to say with 100 percent certainty that it was Andy. The report used the phrase Graves hated most: *"Inconclusive."*

She leaned back in her chair and rubbed her dry tired eyes. Weeks of work. Interviews, surveillance, DNA testing, shoeprint comparisons, false leads, and psychological profiles, and still, she was no closer to the unshakable truth than she had been when Randy Guillaume's body was found in his own gravel driveway. Her office door opened without a knock. District Attorney Whitaker stepped inside, his tie was askew, and his jaw was tight with impatience. He didn't sit. He just hovered. "Melinda," he said flatly, "I just read the latest report." Graves nodded, tapping her pen against her notepad. She said, "It's thin, and it adds a little weight to what we already had." "It doesn't add anything admissible," he said. "A blurry photo, unconfirmed identity, and a kid in proximity? It's not enough. Not for a grand jury. Not for a judge."

Graves looked up at him with angst written all over her face. "You think Marie's confession is legit?" she asked. "I think Marie's dying," Whitaker said, with his voice low. "I think she confessed, and the murder weapon was recovered exactly where she said it'd be. I think the bandana with Andy's DNA is easily explained as an item they shared; handled by both. And I think the court-appointed public defender is already drafting a plea agreement that puts Marie behind bars without ever seeing trial." "She's covering for him," Graves said. "Probably," he responded. Graves pleaded, "Then let me push harder. The boy's cracking. He's carrying something too heavy. I can feel it. The moment she's gone..." "She's not gone yet," Whitaker cut in sharply, "And until she is, we've got a confession, a weapon, motive, and no counter-narrative. No witnesses. No prints. No hard evidence placing Andy at the scene. That's not a case, Graves. That's a hunch." Graves stood now too. She said sarcastically, "So we just close it? File it under 'sacrificial mothers and invisible boys' and move on?" Whitaker exhaled long and slow, "I didn't say it feels good. But it's the law. And our job isn't to chase ghosts. It's to build cases that hold up in court. This one doesn't." He stepped back toward the door, then paused and said, "You did good work. But it's time." And then he left. The door clicked shut behind him.

Graves didn't move for a long time. She stared again at the photo, the blurred outline of a boy in the dark, bandana slung low, like he thought hiding his face could hide everything. And maybe, just maybe, it had. She closed the case file slowly, almost reverently, as if it were still breathing and she hated to suffocate it. Then she turned off the monitor.

Back at his uncle Mark's house, Andy sat on the edge of the twin bed that didn't feel like his. The walls were bare except for a cross above the door and a dusty old photo of Mark in his high school football uniform. The air was heavy with silence. He clutched his sketchpad in both hands but hadn't drawn in days. Mark passed the doorway carrying a tray with two sandwiches and two cans of soda. "You hungry?" he asked gently. Andy nodded, "A little." Mark set the tray down and sat beside him. "I know you miss her," he said, not forcing the conversation, just offering it. Andy nodded again. He didn't have the words, just the weight. Mark put a hand on the boy's shoulder, "She did what she thought was right. And maybe that's all any of us can do." Andy's throat tightened. Was it right? He didn't know anymore. He only knew that it was over. Or so they said. But the truth still lived inside him. A coiled thing. Heavy and quiet like a snake under a rock. He wondered if it would ever let him go.

Graves stayed late that night, past the shift change. Past when her inbox stopped filling up and the hallway outside went still. She stared out the window over the city with one hand resting on the photo folder. "Let it go," Whitaker had said. But some truths never let go of you. Not completely. Not ever.

CHAPTER 27

The Last Light

It had been thirty-two days since Marie Guillaume accepted the plea deal. It was second-degree murder. She was sentenced to thirty years, with medical release contingent on her terminal diagnosis. A legal formality, the DA had called it. She wouldn't survive another three months, let alone make it past processing. It was a deal made on paper, for a punishment that would never come. They transferred her to the medical wing of the women's correctional center outside St. Gabriel, Louisiana. Not to the cellblock and not the general population. Just a white room with a recliner bed, a narrow window, and the sterile hum of distant machines. It was the same as Hospice, but by another name. Marie never asked what the plea said about her legacy. She didn't care how the world saw her anymore. She only cared how Andy did.

When Detective Graves came to see her again, her third visit in as many weeks, Marie was smaller than before. She wasn't just thinner, but dimmer, like her presence was slowly draining from the room. "You don't have to keep coming," Marie said with a faint smile as Graves pulled up a chair. "I know," Graves replied, "But I want to." They sat for a while. The silence was thick with the kind of mutual respect born from hard decisions and quiet truths. "You still don't believe me, do you?" Marie asked softly. Her voice was raspy. "I still believe you're protecting someone," Graves said, "Always have." Marie didn't answer. She just looked toward the window. A breeze stirred the blinds, and for a moment, it almost felt like freedom. "They said I have maybe a month left," Marie said, "Maybe less." "I'm sorry," Graves said. Marie gave a soft shrug, "I'm not. Not anymore. I got to do one thing right." Graves leaned forward, elbows on her knees, "You know they're going to close the case once you're gone." Marie nodded, "That's the point." "There are still things that don't add up," Graves said, "The bandana. The shoeprint. The timeline." Marie met her eyes at that moment, and though her face was pale and worn, there was something sharp still alive in her expression. "I told you the truth," she said, "Maybe not all the pieces, but the part that mattered. And he's free. That's what matters." Graves didn't argue. Not this time. She stayed a few more minutes. She asked about the pain, about the staff, about whether Marie had called anyone else. Marie said no. Andy was it. He was her only connection. He was her only reason. When Graves stood to leave, Marie touched her hand briefly, "Don't let the system swallow him up," she whispered. "He's more than what happened." Graves nodded, "I know."

Andy sat on the floor of his uncle's den with his legs crossed, and with a half-finished sketch in front of him. It was the tree again, the oak tree, the one from the woods behind the Everett's place. But this version was different. This one was hollowed out with branches stripped bare and leaves falling like feathers in a gentle breeze. He hadn't gone to school that day. Mark hadn't forced the issue. When the call came that morning from the prison nurse, Mark had simply turned off the stove, turned to Andy, and said, "You should sit down." She was gone. Marie had lost her battle with cancer. There was no more suffering, and no dramatic goodbye. It was just a slow fade, like a candle left too long in the wind. Andy hadn't cried; at least not yet. And certainly not in front of Mark. He didn't know how to. Especially not for something like this. It wasn't just grief, it was confusion. Relief wrapped in barbed wire. Guilt draped in silence. He kept replaying her last words to him in his head, the final time he'd visited her. "You're going to grow past this," she'd whispered. "I won't be here to see it, but you will. You'll outlive it. That's how you win." He hadn't answered then. He hadn't been able to. Now he wished he had. Mark walked in quietly and handed Andy a folded envelope. "The hospital courier dropped this off. It's from your mom." Andy opened it slowly. Inside was a letter. Her handwriting was shaky but legible:

My boy,

If you're reading this, it means I'm finally resting. No more pain. I'm not scared anymore. And I need you not to be either. I know what I took from you. A confession you never had to make. But, I know what I gave you too. A chance. That's what mothers do when they finally get the courage to.

You were braver than me, Andy. Braver than anyone ever gave you credit for. What you did that night...you did to protect me. I know that. But I also know what it cost you.

You don't have to carry the weight of it forever. Just for now. Just long enough to heal. One day, when you're strong enough, if you still feel like the truth needs to come out...then let it. But only if it sets you free, not if it chains you tighter.

I love you more than anything I've ever known.

Mom

Andy stared at the words for a long time. Then he folded the letter, placed it in the back of his sketchbook, and finally let the tears come, quiet, slow, and unstoppable.

At the Baton Rouge precinct, Graves sat at her desk staring at the, now official, case file. Case disposition: closed. Graves tapped her pen on the file, then closed it. She looked out the window at the dimming sky. There was no joy in the resolution. There was no triumph. There was only stillness. But even stillness had weight. And sometimes, accepting the quiet was the loudest thing you could do.

CHAPTER 28

Echoes and Pages

The truth never left him. It didn't haunt Andy the way it once had; not like it did in those first heavy years after Marie passed. But it stayed close, like an old scar beneath the skin. Some mornings, he'd wake up and forget it existed. Other days, he'd feel the weight of it just behind his ribs. It was a bitter reminder that some storms don't end; they just pass.

Andy grew up under the steady hand of his Uncle Mark. There were rough stretches though. There were silent dinners, school suspensions, and a stretch of teenage rebellion that ran hard and angry. But Mark never gave up on him. He never pushed him for answers he wasn't ready to give. Instead, he gave Andy something he hadn't known how to name back then: *stability and safety*. And always, unconditional love.

Mark was there when Andy graduated high school, when he took night classes at Baton Rouge Community College, when he eventually transferred to Louisiana State University to study literature and psychology. Up to that point in time, he never told anyone about the murder; at least not fully. Not even Mark. The story stayed folded deep inside him, too heavy to lift, and too dangerous to share. But he was able to channel it. First into poems and then into stories. And eventually, into something even larger. At thirty-two years old, Andy published his debut novella. It was called *The Quiet Storm*. He followed that book up with a sequel called *The Quiet Reckoning*. Both were fictionalized accounts, he claimed. A story about a boy who protected his mother, and a mother who took the fall for her boy. The names were changed and so was the ending, but anyone who looked close enough could see the truth breathing through the lines.

The books became bestsellers, which was a surprise to Andy, because they weren't flashy. They weren't explosive. Some critics called them "haunting and inhumane." Readers called them "the kind of story that stays with you." Somewhere out there, Andy figured, Detective Graves must have read them. Maybe, she even recognized bits and pieces of the story. Maybe not. Either way, he didn't write it for her. He wrote it for the version of himself that had once laid in a shelter bed at thirteen years old, staring at the ceiling, wondering if the truth would ever stop burning a hole through his chest.

Andy never wrote a full confession. But in time, his story was the confession. He got married at thirty-five to a quiet, kind woman named Jackie. She was a social worker, strong in spirit and soft in voice. She didn't press him about his past. When she read his books, she only said, "That must have been a hard childhood," and she let him decide how much to say. Andy didn't talk much about Marie to others. But when his daughter turned twelve, when she started asking deeper questions, he told her the story. Not the edited version, but the real one. He told her about the bruises, about the silence, and about the choice. And then he told her how one life-altering moment didn't have to define her entire future. He told her how surviving meant more than just staying alive. It meant learning how to live.

On his seventy-third birthday, Andy sat in a rocking chair on the porch of his modest home in Prairieville, Louisiana. The sun had just started to sink behind the trees, casting long orange shadows over the grass. His great-grandson was playing on the front patio with a wooden airplane, making soft engine sounds and darting it through the air. Inside, Jackie was humming to a pot of gumbo on the stove. The world was quiet, the way he liked it.

There was a bookshelf in his study now, filled with copies of *The Quiet Storm* and *The Quiet Reckoning* and the four books that had followed them. Each book told different stories; some fiction, some not. But they all shared the same heartbeat: the ache of what we carry, and the power of what we choose to release. A reporter once asked him if the boy in his first two books had ever really found peace. Andy just smiled and answered, "He found a life. Sometimes that's the same thing."

Now, he watched his great-grandson launch the plane into the sky. He watched it fall gently to the earth, then saw the boy run to pick it up without a single complaint. And he thought about Marie. He thought about her strength, her sacrifice, and her final letter. He kept it still, in a locked drawer, tucked behind some old photographs and letters he'd never sent. He'd memorized every word. *"You don't have to carry the weight of it forever." "Just long enough to heal."* And he had healed; not perfectly, not easily, but he had. Andy Collins was a husband, a father, a grandfather, and an author who lived a life built from broken pieces. And somehow, he made something whole from it. Not because he forgot, but because he remembered. And he chose to keep going anyway.

About the Author

A.W. Collins is an independent author whose work explores the quiet corners of the human experience, where pain, love, and redemption intersect. Blending realism with emotional truth, A.W. Collins writes stories that confront hardship with unflinching honesty and empathy.

Born with a storyteller's instinct and a poet's sensitivity, A.W. Collins has penned two novellas and a book of poetry, each reflecting a lifelong fascination with resilience; the strength that carries us through loss, guilt, and change.

When not writing, A.W. Collins continues to pursue creative growth and personal renewal, turning life's struggles into art that resonates with readers who have fought their own battles and found meaning in the reckoning. *The Quiet Reckoning* is both a story and a reflection of that journey. Though fictional, it is an exploration of what it means to be broken, forgiven, and free.

Author's Reflection

Writing fiction has given me the freedom to transform pieces of a difficult past into something meaningful. Through story, I can give shape to feelings that once had no voice - fear, anger, confusion, and loss - and turn them into characters who struggle, endure, and eventually find their own strength. Fiction has allowed me to revisit those early emotions without being trapped by them, to reinterpret pain through imagination rather than memory.

In many ways, each story I write is both an act of healing and of honesty. The line between truth and invention blurs, but what remains real are the emotions that drive it. Writing has become a way to reclaim the parts of my childhood that were shaped by instability and hardship, and to turn them into something that might speak to others who've faced their own storms.

Fiction, for me, isn't an escape; it's a reckoning. It's how I make peace with the past while giving life to the lessons it left behind. *The Quiet Storm* and *The Quiet Reckoning* are not a retelling of my life, but they are shaped by the ache of loss, the search and desire for redemption, and the quiet strength it takes to move forward. Writing these books has reminded me that even the hardest chapters of life can lead to somewhere hopeful.

-A.W. Collins

www.ingramcontent.com/pod-product-compliance
Lightning Source LLC
Chambersburg PA
CBHW021234130726
47988CB00002B/968